Lame Dog Murder

By the same author

THREE FOR ADVENTURE
FOUR FIND DANGER
TWO MEET TROUBLE
HEIR TO MURDER
MURDER COMES HOME
WHO SAW HIM DIE?
MURDER BY THE WAY
FOUL PLAY SUSPECTED
CRIME WITH MANY VOICES
FIVE TO KILL
MURDER AT KING'S KITCHEN
MURDER MAKES MURDER
NO CRIME MORE CRUEL
WHO DIES AT THE GRANGE?
WHO SAID MURDER?
MYSTERY MOTIVE
LEND A HAND TO MURDER
NO END TO DANGER
FIRST A MURDER
WHO KILLED REBECCA?
THE DYING WITNESSES
MURDER WEEK-END
DINE WITH MURDER
QUARREL WITH MURDER
TAKE A BODY

A Falcon's Head Mystery

Lame Dog Murder

John Creasey

WORLD PUBLISHING

TIMES MIRROR

NEW YORK

Published by The World Publishing Company
Published simultaneously in Canada
by Nelson, Foster & Scott Ltd.
First American edition
First printing—1972
First published in Great Britain in 1952
All rights reserved
ISBN 0-529-04481-1
Library of Congress catalog card number: 70-185119
Printed in the United States of America

WORLD PUBLISHING
TIMES MIRROR

CONTENTS

1.	Brothers at Home	7
2.	First Lame Dog	15
3.	Puzzle	24
4.	Caller for Clarke	31
5.	Mystery Man	38
6.	Barbara	46
7.	Rosa	54
8.	The Maestro	62
9.	News	70
10.	Squeak	78
11.	Scotland Yard	86
12.	"Where's Richard?"	95
13.	Kidnapped?	102
14.	Ribley Court	110
15.	Murder	117
16.	Family Conference	126
17.	The Assistant Commissioner	135
18.	Police Cell	141
19.	Two Missing	150
20.	Rosa's Future	156

21. WARNING   163

22. BLANK WALL?   171

23. DIVERSION?   179

24. KELBY RAVES   186

25. WISE RENNIE   194

26. GOOD NEWS FOR HENDERSON   202

27. THE TRUTH ABOUT HENDERSON   208

28. FANE FAMILY   216

I

" You don't mean to tell me that you're going to be in to-night," said Martin Fane, looking at his brother, who was standing in front of some corner bookshelves and fingering books one after the other.

" I am—home life for me in future." Richard Fane glanced round, and gave a most attractive grin. " That is, if I shan't be in the way. Tell me, and I'll be out the moment Barbara comes. I wouldn't play gooseberry. Just say shoo and I'll shoo."

Martin brushed a lock of straight hair from his broad forehead, settled back more comfortably in a large arm-chair, which he filled, kept a solemn face, but let his grey eyes twinkle.

" That means you're broke."

" Have I asked you to lend me money? " Richard took out a hefty volume bound in green, and carried it to an arm-chair on the other side of the electric fire. " The trouble with you is native scepticism. Because my job often takes me out in the evening, you assume I don't like home life. My boy, you're wrong. Shoes off, slippers on, a stool to put the old feet on, a good book, and amiable company. What more could a man want? "

" Night life. A hideous cacophony, miscalled music. Stuffy atmosphere, blondes reeking of cheap scent, and everything that goes with it. Or back-stage at the theatre, or this society function or that. Anywhere the liquor's free or cheap and the company dubious."

Martin picked up a folded copy of *The Times*, but did not look at it. Richard whistled softly, smoothed down his curly hair—it was brown, like his brother's, the only

7

point of similarity between the two, except for a good, fresh complexion—and let the hefty tome fall heavily on to a table by his side. He was nearly as tall as Martin, but lean and wiry, whereas Martin was big and bulky. His face was narrow and Martin's broad; and his ears stuck out. That gave a homely touch to a ridiculously handsome face. Just now, his large blue eyes had the innocent candour of a child's.

"My dear Scoop! That what you really think of me?"

"Sometimes."

"Unjust. You know, old chap, I wish you wouldn't sit back and criticize me to yourself and say nothing about it. Oh, I know you've said plenty to-night, but it's always like that. Long periods of silence and then a blitzkrieg. Being the strong silent man may suit you, but is it fair? Is it just? I ask you?"

"Yes."

"I suppose you mean it's the only way to lead a peaceful life. Perhaps you're right. My skin's thin, at times. To-night I'm in a sorrowful, almost a soulful mood, though; I think I can take anything. Well, nearly anything, don't pitch it too hard. What *do* you think of my goings on?"

Martin deliberated, and his eyes continued to twinkle. He did most things deliberately, and seldom acted without having considered all the likely consequences of any course of action. Richard, on the other hand, was impulsive to a fault. He lit a cigarette, while Martin fondled the warm bowl of a large pipe.

"Don't take all night," said Richard, almost sharply. "What do you think of them?"

Martin uttered one word. "Silly."

Richard flushed.

"No, hang it. It *is* my job. I'm doomed to do the gossip column in a chatty weekly, and a man must live. I can't say I like it, but it has to be done—I sponge on you quite enough as it is."

8

"You could use your job as an excuse," Martin murmured.

"Meaning, I like the gay life?"

"Gay!"

"That is the accepted term," said Richard moodily. "Well, up to a point, yes. But I get sick of it. I don't mind telling you, Scoop, that I'm sick of my job. It's a queer thing, at home the Maestro sits back and reels stuff off in his sleep, as it were. The golden words spill from his typewriter. I thought I'd inherited his talent, but I think it was a mistake. I feel squarish in a round hole, but what else am I good for? Journalism's something, after all."

"What you lack is the Maestro's capacity for hard work. Things come too easily to you, you don't have to try enough."

Richard scowled.

"I certainly asked for it, so don't pull your punches."

"I'm not punching," said Martin almost lazily. "Just trying to make you sit up and take notice. I think you're right about one thing, your present job isn't any good to you. You don't really like it, but it's easy and smooth and you meet a lot of nonentities who get in the limelight, and it's nice to be ogled by film stars because you might get them a few inches in a newspaper."

"Not *punching*," breathed Richard. "Generally speaking, I have no time for film stars. Most of those I meet are only starlets, anyhow. Of course, now and again I meet a nice, homely type of girl who's getting along nicely, but they're soon spoiled." He brightened up. "You know, I've often thought of having a shot at writing a scenario. I met Arnold Battley the other day, and was talking to him about it. He said he'd gladly read anything I wrote. Influential chap, Battley, and——"

"How many days ago was it when you met him?"

"Eh? What's to-day—Thursday? Would be Monday. Or Sunday. Why?"

9

" If it was Sunday he'd forgotten you on Monday, if it was Monday he'd forgotten you on Tuesday."

" Ha-ha," said Richard scornfully. " Martin Fane, the great cynic. For a man of your tremendous capacity for taking pains and a great mind to bend on life, you haven't exactly hit the ceiling yet, have you? At twenty-six, rising twenty-seven, you're still a junior cartoonist for an advertising agency where, they say, there's plenty of scope for advancement. True, you make a couple of hundred a year more than I, but——"

He stopped, for Martin was smiling amiably.

" Sorry, old chap. No need for me to be spiteful! " Richard jumped up. " Have a beer? "

" Thanks. Why say spiteful? You were on the mark. I'm as tired of Merridew's as you're tired of the *Charade*. Ever thought of going into business together? "

Richard, standing by the wall-cupboard where they kept the beer and all other drinks, turned round as if stung. Martin's smile remained.

" *What?* "

" You heard."

" Are you serious? "

" Yes."

Richard took out two bottles of beer, two silver tankards —presents for their twenty-first birthdays—opened the bottles and poured out. He carried a tankard to Martin, placed it slowly and firmly into his hand, backed away, and said :

" You're drunk. Good health."

They drank.

" Not yet," said Martin equably. " Drunk, I mean."

" My dear chap! Think what you're saying. I am the feckless younger son of a famous fictioneer, spoiled in my teens, without a sane idea in my head, lazy, girl-crazy, hypnotized by film stars. Remember? Anyone who was daft enough to start business with me would be taking on a liability from the first. Didn't anyone tell you? "

"Who said you never have ideas?"

Richard went to his chair, sat down, lit another cigarette, and spoke in a more serious voice.

"How long have you been thinking about this?"

"For the past few months. I'd have talked about it earlier, but I couldn't think what line would suit us best. Neither of us enjoys working for a boss, and I think we'd both do better as our own masters. We mustn't start anything that needs a lot of capital. The Maestro would let us have anything within reason, of course, or we could draw on the capital he gave us a few years ago, but—well, we couldn't really call this a rainy day. In any case I'd rather start from scratch."

"Mutton-head," said Richard. "What you mean is, living in the shadow of the Maestro has its drawbacks, you doubt if either of us would have our present jobs if it weren't for his reflected glory, and—you're right, too! On the other hand, he'd probably jump at the chance to finance us, if he thought the business had prospects. If I know him, he'd want his cut in profits, too! Strictly a business undertaking. He might even be glad to lose a bit, he could save on income tax."

"What a mind you have!"

"Why blink at facts?" Richard put down his beer and looked very thoughtful—and hopeful. "Out with it, Scoop. You wouldn't have started this if you hadn't a pretty shrewd idea what you want to do. Advertising agency? News agency? Special features stuff? When you come to think of it, that's about all we're qualified for. Which is your choice?"

"None of them."

Richard considered this for some time in silence, and then observed:

"Then I'm stymied. What else could we turn our hands to? You've always hankered after architecture or something like that, but I'd be a useless partner, I just can't get the staircase in the right place." He snorted. "Remember the time when the Maestro asked me to do a sketch of a flat for him, for one of the masterpieces? No one noticed what was wrong until after the book was published, when he had ninety-seven fan letters pointing out that he'd forgotten the bathroom and W.C. Poor old Dad! Not a word of reproach, said he blamed himself for not checking it more closely. Mother gave me a piece of her mind, and before I knew where I was he was defending me fiercely. How he loves lame dogs! He——"

" You've got it," said Martin. He hadn't moved, except for the rhythmic rise and fall of his right arm.

Richard looked puzzled.

" Got what? "

" The idea."

Richard leaned forward, adjusted the crease of his trousers, peered closely into Martin's eyes, and asked anxiously:

" Haven't been overdoing it lately, have you? Strain does queer things. I knew a chap who was walking about for eight days with concussion and didn't know it. Promised his wife the world. She soon put him right. I mean, you don't want a rest or anything like that, do you? Try a week off. Read some heavy stuff, like this." He tapped the hefty tome. " Why on earth these Russians always wrote as if they'd a life expectancy of a couple of centuries I don't know. *War and Peace*—why write it at all? Still, it can be soothing at the right time, and you read too many of the Maestro's outpourings—not to mention his competitors. A crime story's all right once in a way, but you steep yourself in them. Fact and fiction—it's almost an obsession."

" It is an obsession."

" Once you admit it, half the danger's over," said Richard, as if with relief. " Supposing you have an early night? I'll come and tuck you up. Yes? "

" You've hit the target again," said Martin, his eyes gleaming.

Richard sat back.

" Sorry. I may be blind, but I don't see what I've got. Lame dogs and obsessions don't exactly seem the proper basis for a business. Dad and his helping hand is one thing, but it *costs* him a small fortune. I take it you want to make money? This isn't one of your altruistic notions, is it? Man should not work for profit, but for the benefit of his fellow man."

" You've got the idea wrong, but this isn't altruistic, anyhow."

" I suppose not. After all, you and Barbara *are* engaged, she won't want to marry a man who's constantly dressed in sackcloth and ashes. She——"

" Would be the third partner," said Martin.

" What ! " gasped Richard.

" She has the training, I've a little knowledge, you have some ideas, and you're also the salesman." Martin finished his beer and put the tankard down on the table. " Listen, Skip. Supposing we started a kind of Lame Dog Agency? That is, a kind of general information bureau, guaranteeing quick results. A private inquiry agency with a difference. Not exactly another Universal Aunts' service, but something on those lines. We know our way about the Street, we know how to get at odd pieces of information, we know London inside out—think how a party of bright young things would enjoy you as a guide ! We both know French, too. I believe we could work the thing up. I should put five hundred into it, Barbara would put up two hundred and fifty, and you would have to make it up to the thousand somehow. On that capital I think we could run for a year. Barbara and I have been thinking of it for some months, and it could be made to go."

Martin spoke quietly, but with a feeling and enthusiasm he seldom showed.

" Well, well, well," breathed Richard. " Bring your troubles to us, everything supplied from an elephant to a flea, service with charm, information with a smile. Murder cases solved as a sideline for a special fee. Scoop,

13

Scoop, oh, *Scoop*! I thought I was the crazy member of this family. I——"

The front-door bell rang. Richard looked round abruptly, and jumped up, as if he'd completely forgotten the conversation.

"You stick to drawing! I wonder who this can be. I gather you're not expecting Barbara to-night, can't imagine anyone else calling, can you?" He was a little too casual. "I'll go and see. Won't be a jiff."

He hurried out.

Martin continued to sit back in his chair, filling it comfortably, and drawing at his pipe. He was frowning slightly, and telling himself that Richard had expected a visitor but hadn't wanted to say so. The visitor was almost certainly the reason for his staying indoors.

Richard had left the door open, and his "Why, *hello*!" came clear and warmly—and was followed by a girl's voice.

Richard Fane hurried down the red-carpeted stairs which led to the front door of the flat. The flat was on the top floor of a four-storey building. A door had been put at the foot of the top flight of stairs, and the stairs themselves boarded in. Below were three flights of un-carpeted stairs and a street door alongside the window of a grocer's shop. The narrow street outside was silent; yet less than a hundred yards away was the Strand and the noise and bustle of London's heart.

A girl stood outside.

" Why, hello! " cried Richard, and sounded almost as if he were both surprised and delighted.

" Hallo, Richard." The girl lowered her voice. " Is it all right? "

" I think so." Richard gave a delighted grin. " In fact, very promising. Martin's taken up some crazy notion, and is looking for lame dogs. Mind being a lame dog for to-night? "

" I feel like one," said the girl. " Can he hear? "

" Only a mutter. He won't bite, you know, he's quite human."

Richard raised his voice for the last few words, chuckled, and led the way up the stairs. The bedrooms and kitchen were approached through a doorway opposite the stairs; the living-room, with a dining-alcove off it, was approached through a door on the left. The living-room was long and narrow, furnished comfortably with hide arm-chairs, one or two occasional chairs, an oak gateleg table in the window. Several pleasant water-colours hung on the walls, and there were bookshelves in three corners. The lighting on this March evening came from wall-lamps and a standard lamp between the two hide arm-chairs which were drawn up in front of the fire.

It was nearly nine o'clock.

"Would you believe it!" said Richard, hurrying in behind the girl. "We've a guest. Kathleen—spelt with a K, not a C—this is my brother Martin. Kathleen Wilder, Martin. You've probably heard of her, or seen her on the films. Lucky thing we were in—or lucky that I was, Martin's in much more often. Drink?"

Martin was on his feet, and smiling amiably. Kathleen Wilder was something to smile at even for a man not remarkable for being susceptible to beauty. She was small, nicely dressed in a green coat with a big collar and full sleeves, she wore a small hat of the same material, which allowed much of her auburn hair to show; it was lovely hair, glossy and waving. She had a heart-shaped face, and her complexion was flawless; she had a slight flush, because of the wind outside.

"Hallo, Miss Wilder."

"I've heard a lot about you," said Kathleen Wilder.

"Never believe half Richard says."

"Oh, I don't," said Kathleen, and her eyes sparkled, to match the gleam in Martin's. Martin felt that she would be easy to get on with. "He has warned me about it himself, I must be fair."

"What's this, a conspiracy already?" Richard was at the wall-cupboard. "Gin, sherry, or we could offer——"

"May I have a gin-and-orange?"

"You may."

Richard busied himself, while the girl loosened her coat, for it was warm in here, and sat in one of the smaller chairs which Martin pulled up between the two large ones. She had nice ankles, and her legs were sheathed in nylon stockings. She took off her gloves; her hands were small, white, and shapely—she wore no rings, and only used a pale-pink nail-varnish.

"Kath is in films, of course," said Richard, bringing

16

her drink over. " She's pretty good, too. Much better than directors and producers seem to think."

The girl smiled disarmingly.

" I've been very lucky, really. I've only been in films for a year and have had several small parts."

" Like the life? " asked Martin.

" Here, steady! " Richard looked horrified. " You've given me a dose of how I ought to live, don't start on Kath. She's lucky you're not her brother. Of course she likes it. In a few years' time she's going to be a star, take it from me. The only question is whether they'll recognize it here, or whether she'll have to go to Hollywood."

" As a matter of fact," said Kathleen Wilder, " I don't think I shall ever become a star, I haven't the little some-thing that it needs."

" Good Lord! The modest film actress. Martin, treat her with great care, she's unique. She's also talking a lot of nonsense, of course, she knows she's good, and so do all the discerning critics. But I won't embarrass her any more—nice of you to pop in, Kath. I told her where we lived," added Richard with bland unconcern, " and said we'd always be glad to say hallo if she looked in. She's a near neighbour. That is, she lives over in the Adelphi—or the Adelphi that was. With a friend who "—he grinned—" spends far too much time out with foolish newspapermen because she thinks she can persuade them to give her a few inches in the newspapers. That is, she did, before she found a boy friend. That's probably what she was after. Some of these girls! "

He had poured out more beer, and sat down.

" It *does* get a bit wearisome, being alone every night," said Kathleen.

" As if Martin doesn't know! "

" Listen," said Martin lazily, " this was all on. Noth-ing would normally keep Richard in during the evening unless he's ill, and if he's ill to-night it's a mental illness no one can do anything about. There were the conspira-

17

torial whispers at the door. Why take the trouble? Any friend of Richard's is welcome."

Richard made a face.

" Humbug. The last time we had a few friends of mine here, I had to restrain you from throwing them out."

" There were five, and they didn't arrive until one o'clock in the morning."

" One day you'll have to meet our father," said Richard solemnly. " He's the only other man in the world with an answer for everything. Martin takes after him, except that he can't write the golden words. As a matter of fact, Scoop, I did suggest that Kath should look in to-night if she were free."

He began to grin and then to chuckle, and the girl as well as Martin looked at him uncomprehendingly. He chuckled for a long time, obviously really amused.

" Richard——" began Kathleen.

" Sorry. I'll stop. You took the wind out of my sails to-night, brother—otherwise I would have told you. You see, Kath's a "—he chuckled again—" a lame dog. Oh, Lord! Is it funny? "

" Very," said Martin dryly.

" Our very first lame dog. And——"

" Mr. Fane——" began Kathleen, to Martin.

" Oh, no," pleaded Richard. " You may call him Martin, I give permission. Let's all be friends."

" Mr. Fane," repeated Kathleen, " I told Richard that I didn't see any point in making a mystery of it, but he seemed to think you'd be more interested if I pretended to come by chance. I was talking to him about it this morning—I doubt if I should have, except that I know what your father does."

" Maestro of the twanging nerve," breathed Richard.

" Is Richard *always* like this?" Kathleen asked.

" Nearly always."

" Try to be quiet for two minutes, Richard," said Kathleen. " You see, it's a mystifying business, and I

18

don't know what to do about it. It may only be a trifle, I suppose it *is*, but——"

" Sorry," said Richard. " Wrong approach. In a minute you'll be saying that it's like a plot in one of the Maestro's stories. Martin's nearly as allergic as the Maestro himself to other people offering plots for crime stories. Kind suggestions roll off me, but they both start taking suggestions seriously, and then find that they've wasted a lot of time and the plot won't work out."

" Martin," said Kathleen firmly, " we've lost our dog."

Martin started violently. Richard grinned almost from ear to ear, raised his tankard as in a toast, and drank. Kathleen sat still and looked demure, with the glass of gin-and-orange in her hand, and her fine hazel eyes fixed on Martin. He recovered from the shock of surprise, and said lamely:

" I'm sorry about that."

" It's a very fine dog. A Pekinese." Richard screwed up his face. " Yap-yap-yap-yap, but *very* affectionate. Slightly lame in the nearside hind leg, too! "

" When you get to know Pekes you like them," said Kathleen firmly. " It isn't mine, I wouldn't keep a dog in a flat, it's my friend's—Rosa's." She was obviously bothered, and talked disjointedly; Richard didn't help by sitting back and grinning. " The thing is, we live in a flat opposite another flat. I mean——"

Richard held out his hands, a foot apart.

" One flat here. One flat there."

" Be quiet! It's at the top of a house in Buckley Street, there's a flat on each side at the top. You walk across a narrow landing, and the doors are opposite each other. Ours is Number 6. The woman at the flat opposite often took Ching—that's the dog—for a walk. He would wander into her flat, he was almost common property." Kathleen was now talking swiftly, and Richard was smiling only faintly. " He wandered over there two days ago. I know she let him in and said she'd look after him, but— he's never come out. At least, I don't think he has.

The first night Rosa and I were out late, there was a film première and a party, and we took it for granted the neighbour had kept Ching for the night. When he didn't turn up yesterday I went to ask if he was there. The woman's husband answered the door, said his wife was away for a few days, and that he hadn't seen Ching. He was quite sure Ching hadn't gone with her, as he saw her off at the station. But—Ching's disappeared. He's never disappeared before, even for an hour or two, he wouldn't even go down the stairs unless one of us was with him. I was at a cocktail party this morning, and was talking to Richard. I told him, and he said——"

" Stop," said Richard firmly.

" I will not stop. He said that you were exactly the man for a problem like this, you would immediately evolve a dozen different theories and find Ching in no time. You see, we don't like going to the police, it almost looks as if we're accusing Mrs. Clarke——"

" That's the neighbour," interpolated Richard.

" Yes. Of stealing him. Anyhow, that's what Rosa says, and she won't go to the police although she's worried. You hear so much about horrible things happening to dogs that are stolen, don't you? "

" Not much meat on a Peke," said Richard.

" Richard, don't be beastly."

" Sorry. But do you? I mean, is there? "

" Ignore him," said Martin. " As a matter of fact, that's what you ought to have done from the beginning. He's the man of crazy ideas. When he suggested that you should come and talk to me about it, he was talking out of the back of his neck. I'd like to help, but I don't see what I can do."

" Feet of clay," groaned Richard.

" Quite honestly, nor do I," said Kathleen. " I don't even know what one does when starting to look for a lost dog. Rosa says she would advertise in the *Evening News*, but is it worth it? From the point of view of getting results, I mean? "

" Certainly not." Richard leaned forward and pressed the tips of his fingers together. " It was a bright idea to bring you here, even before to-night. It proved I've a sixth sense. Martin has a notion that he could set himself up as a kind of Personal Problems Agency. Scoop, solve this one, and I'll beg, borrow, or steal my share of the capital! There's a nice challenge for you. What has happened to King Ching, the Prize Peke of the Adelphi? Rosa was training him, too. She's decided that she has no future herself on the screen, but knows that a good doggy actor is worth a fortune. He has a leg that doesn't work properly, too, makes him limp appealingly. I must say he was an intelligent little creature, and this is a pretty problem. Solve it."

" After all," said Kathleen earnestly, " you did help to solve that other mystery, didn't you? It was in all the papers. You carried a body round in the back of your car without knowing it was in there. I know this isn't the same, but——"

She broke off in some confusion. Richard was looking at her thoughtfully now, and not smiling. Martin's eyes had lost their twinkle; he looked ruggedly handsome and impressive. He brushed back the lock of hair, glanced from one to the other, and wondered what really lay behind all this. He had felt sure that Richard had simply wanted to bring Kathleen to the flat, probably to get his opinion of her, and that had suggested that Richard was more serious about her than he had been about any-one else. That idea faded—it didn't go completely, but was much less vivid. There was something else, certainly in the girl's mind. She hadn't come here because of a missing Pekinese—or at least, not only because of a missing Pekinese. Richard might have known that; might have suspected it; or might have realized it at the same time as Martin, and now be thinking ruefully that yet another bright notion had recoiled on him.

" Taking the case? " Richard asked quietly.

" Not yet," said Martin firmly. " Half a story is no

good. What's really worrying you, Kathleen? You've come because you are worried and don't want to go to the police, but it isn't just about Ching. Is it?"

Richard pursed his lips, and then said:

"You can't fool Martin. And he calls a spade a spade and a pretty girl a liar without batting an eye. I wish I had his skin, it's as thick as armour plating. As the secret's out, though, I'll confess I thought there was more in it than a doggy story; that's why I thought it would be a good idea to try it out on Big Brother. I thought he'd shout 'no', I didn't know he was plotting a new career."

As he stopped, Kathleen looked from one to the other, eyes bright and cheeks flushed. Martin's smile could hardly have been more reassuring. She smiled back, opened her mouth—and the telephone bell rang.

"You're nearest," said Richard promptly. "Confound the thing, its inventor ought to be pole-axed."

Martin was able to reach the telephone without getting up. He put the receiver to his ear, with a quiet "Sorry," to Kathleen Wilder, and wished the interruption hadn't come then. "Hallo? This is Temple Bar 88951."

A woman cried, "*Is Kath Wilder there?*"

It wasn't just a quiet inquiry, but a shout which sounded through the room. Martin moved the earpiece farther from his ear; the woman would probably shout again.

"Yes. Who is that?"

"Tell her she must come home at once. It's Rosa, tell her she must come! Something amazing——"

The woman at the other end broke off; it might have been an exclamation of distress, it might have been a cry of alarm. She put the receiver down noisily. Obviously the others had heard that, and Kathleen was getting up, Richard was frowning at his brother.

"*Was* that Rosa?" Kathleen demanded. "I left this telephone number, she was nervous."

22

" It was Rosa, and she wants you back because something amazing has happened," said Martin. " Get our coats, Skip, will you? Kathleen, what is all this about? "

"We must hurry," said Kathleen. " I'll tell you on the way."

3

THE Fane brothers kept their car on a waste patch of land near the flat. It was a powerful cream-coloured Buick, in the luggage-boot of which a body had once been hidden, as Kathleen knew. Five minutes after getting the message, all three were sitting on the front seat, and Martin was at the wheel; Kathleen sat next to him. Both men were hatless. A fierce wind struck down the narrow street. When the headlights went on, they shone upon the windows of publishing houses, a few shop signs, and two blank walls. The car purred along towards the Strand, was held up by cross traffic, and was likely to be delayed for several minutes; the Strand was undergoing one of its periodical repairs.

" Time to talk," Richard said.

" There isn't much, it's all so vague," said Kathleen. " Everything I've told you is true, but when I went to ask Mr. Clarke, he nearly snapped my head off. Told me to keep the little beast out of his flat, he didn't approve of his wife having anything to do with it. He's always been rather mousy, we haven't seen him very often. I don't think Rosa's ever seen him. His wife's a rather faded little woman, she must have been lovely once, but the life's almost drained out of her. As a matter of fact, Rosa and I felt sorry for her, that's why we allowed Ching to go over so often. She was alone a great deal, and she found him company—it suited us both very well."

The traffic eased; Martin drove across. The neon lights on the tall buildings near Trafalgar Square spread different colours over the sky. The wind howled down the Strand, people were clutching at their hats, a few

24

cyclists were having to pedal heavily, and kept their heads down.

The Buick slid down a narrow street leading to the Adelphi and some of the roads there which looked exactly as they had when they had been built in the time of the Regency. Tall, narrow houses, once all private homes, now temporary office premises—until the big rebuilding scheme could be set properly under way.

" Yes," said Martin.

" It's first right, then second left," said Kathleen. " Well—we couldn't understand why Mr. Clarke should fly into a temper. And it was a puzzle about his wife. The last time we saw her she said that she'd hoped they would get away for a holiday soon, but her husband had said it was impossible. And the last time she did go away for a week-end—nearly a year ago—she was preparing for it for weeks, couldn't talk about anything else. I suppose——"

Martin turned second left.

" It's half-way down on the right, just past that lamp," said Kathleen. " I suppose the truth is, Clarke rather scared us. I don't suppose we should have thought twice about it, but for Ching. If Clarke had just thrown him out, he would have been waiting outside our door, and we're sure he went in. She promised to look after him, as I told you. Rosa was nervous about it—she's rather a nervous type—and, well, the whole thing got out of proportion. I didn't tell Richard all this, but I was angling for a chance to talk to you both about it. I honestly don't know anyone to consult about a thing like this. We shouldn't be justified in going to the police, should we? "

" Not yet," said Martin. " This right? "

" This will do, it's the second house along now."

They drew up outside the house. There was a light at a front window on the first floor, but the rest of the building was in darkness. Kathleen glanced up as if she had expected to see a light at the top window, but she didn't speak. She led the way, and her fingers were unsteady when she started to put the key in the lock. Richard took it from her, opened the door, and looked into darkness.

Kathleen said, " That's funny."

" What's funny? "

" The landing lights are out. There are six flats here, and we all agree to have the lights on each landing until midnight, and one on after that."

" Someone's forgotten to switch them on," said Richard.

" It's not that. They were on when I left, just after eight o'clock."

" Nip back and get the torch, Martin, will you? " asked Richard.

He flicked his lighter, went forward, and put out a hand towards the light switches near a door. Before he touched them Martin said firmly:

" Leave those. You get the torch, will you? "

" Why——" began Richard, and then gulped. " Oh, I see. Great man on the trail, finger-prints might be smeared. Yes, sir. Nuisance I forgot my gloves."

Martin seldom wore gloves, anyhow. Richard slid past them towards the car, and Martin and the girl stood in the dark, narrow hallway. A little light came in from the street; just enough to show them the stairs and the shape of two doors. There was no sound, except at the car.

Richard came back, flashing a powerful torch.

" Just follow me," he said.

The torch shone up the carpeted stairs; they were narrow, with wooden banisters which gleamed dark brown. The walls, papered cream, were quite blank. The stairs creaked a little as they went up and reached the first landing—the light at the front window was at this level.

" It can't be much," Martin said. " These people are in, aren't they? "

" The man's—deaf," said Kathleen in a small voice.

26

" He's elderly, and as deaf as a post. The flat opposite him and below us is empty, it's being decorated, and the ground-floor people are usually out in the evening."

" Just like me," said Richard.

" Don't joke," said Kathleen sharply.

Martin glanced at her profile in the faint light which spread about the landing. It was a nice profile, and her expression was set; the girl was really nervous. Richard led the way quickly up the stairs, and Martin held the girl's arm. They reached the top landing, and Richard said:

" No harm in switching on, is there, if I use a handker-chief to hold the switch? " He took a handkerchief from his pocket and pressed a switch down. Light came on above their heads, mellowed by a parchment shade.

" All in working order. All quiet, too."

" Which is your flat? " Martin asked.

Kathleen pointed to the one farther away from the head of the stairs, and which was reached by a yard-wide passage, little more than a bridge. Number 6 was painted on it.

" There. I expected Rosa to be waiting at the door."

" She probably had an attack of jitters," said Richard. " Let me have the key."

" Better knock or ring first," said Martin. " She might get scared if we just walk in."

" She's expecting Kathleen, hang it," said Richard. He rang the bell, all the same, and it sounded louder—a battery type, with the bell itself just inside the door. They all stood still, and there was no other sound, no light shining at the bottom or sides of the doors.

" Rosa's not deaf, is she? " asked Richard.

" Richard, please."

" Sorry. Key? "

She held it out, but before Richard could take it, Martin took it from her fingers, and slipped past Richard to the door. Richard gave a crooked grin, and stood back. Martin opened the door slowly; no light came through.

The others stepped forward, close on his heels. He went inside, asking:

" Is there a hall? "

" No, just a narrow entrance to the living-room. The light's on the right."

Martin could just see the switch, and used a handkerchief to touch it and press down. The light came on, showing a long, narrow room—much narrower than that at the Fanes' flat. It was charming; chintzes and flowers gave it brightness, an upright piano stood at the far end of the room, although it was almost too large. The chairs were small, everything had a pleasant touch about it. The cream-coloured carpet had a deep pile. Three doors led off one side; he guessed that it had once been a large room, and had been turned into a small flat.

Kathleen called weakly, " Rosa."

There was no answer.

" Don't get worried," Richard said, and took her arm protectively. " She probably went out just after telephoning."

" That wasn't much more than ten minutes ago."

" Well, Rosa's a bit unpredictable, isn't she? "

" Not as unpredictable as this," said Kathleen.

" Which is her room? "

Martin was near the first door.

" The next one—that's the kitchen. It's our room, there's only one bedroom." Kathleen drew in a sharp breath. " I don't like it. Why on earth did she go out after telephoning us like that? "

Martin didn't try to answer. Richard used this situation as an excuse to slide an arm round Kathleen's waist. Martin shone the torch round the bedroom, then switched on the light with his elbow. This was a much larger room, with twin beds. The same charm of decor was shown here, and the colouring was pale blue and white. The furniture, of sycamore, gleamed beneath the light which had come on over each bed and over the dressing-table standing between the beds.

" Not here," said Martin briefly. " I'll look in the other rooms."

Kathleen's manner had troubled him; he was almost nervous as he went into the kitchen, on one side of the bedroom, and then into the bathroom, on the other side. There was no sign of Rosa, no message, nothing to suggest where she might have gone.

They all went back to the living-room.

" I wish I could understand it," Kathleen said in a husky voice. " What did she say exactly? "

" Just that this something amazing had happened and she wanted you to come home."

Martin did not add that she had broken off with a sound which might have been a cry of alarm.

" If she went out she'd have put on a coat," said Richard.

" I'll go and see if one's gone."

Kathleen hurried into the bedroom. All the lights in the flat were on now, but there was silence; it was uncanny. It was broken by the opening of the wardrobe door. Richard hesitated for a moment in the bedroom doorway, frowning and looking puzzled, then went into the room. Martin glanced round the flat. He hadn't seen the small table behind a chair, with a glass on it, an ash-tray with several cigarette-ends tipped as with lipstick, and what looked like some white crochet-work. The gas fire was burning gently, and there was a chintz-covered pouf in front of it, as if someone had put her feet on the pouf and been crocheting when disturbed.

The others came back.

" All her coats are there," said Kathleen. " So are all mine. She wouldn't go out on a night like this without a top-coat. She wouldn't be hiding anywhere in the flat."

Kathleen turned her head and looked towards the front door. She didn't say what was in her mind; Martin wondered whether she had told them everything she knew.

29

" Perhaps she was scared and ran across to Clarke for comfort," Richard said.

" Rosa's not easily scared. She might have gone downstairs—yes, she might be downstairs." Kathleen moved quickly towards the door, but stopped before she reached it, and turned round. She stood with her back towards the little recess in front of the door—too short to be called a passage and too small to be called a hall. " But if she'd gone down to Mitchell she would have been waiting and listening for us, and would have come rushing out the moment she knew we'd arrived. I *know* Rosa." Kathleen stopped; then went on in a small voice, " Now I'm really frightened."

Into the silence which followed, and while Richard went across and put his arm round her waist and squeezed reassuringly, there came a heavy knocking on a door.

KATHLEEN jumped, freed herself from Richard, and turned and stared at the door. The knocking was repeated, but it wasn't at this flat. Martin took out his pipe and began to fill it, and Richard said easily:

"Visitor for Mr. Clarke. The lights weren't on in there, were they? He's probably out, too."

The knocking was repeated, and Kathleen walked towards a chair, pulled off her hat, and sat down. Her hair tumbled almost to her shoulders, a surprising amount had been hidden by her hat. She poked her fingers through it, and loosened the top buttons of her coat. She was pale, and looked anxiously towards the door all the time. There was no more knocking, but footsteps came steadily.

Kathleen's hands clenched.

"Look here, you're getting too jumpy," Richard said. "I——" He started, almost as violently as Kathleen, for a sharp ring came at the front door here. He grinned. "I see what you mean. Like me to go, Scoop?"

He didn't move.

Martin went across to the door; his bulk nearly filled the little recess, and he hid whoever was there from sight.

"Good evening."

"Sorry to worry you," said a man with a pleasant voice. "I wondered if Mr. Clarke was here, by any chance. From the flat opposite, I mean."

Martin looked into the face of a tall man—a vaguely familiar face. The man wore a bowler hat, his hair was fair, and the light from behind Martin showed his eyes to be very blue. He wore a blue Melton overcoat with a thick belt, and the collar was turned up, as if against the wind outside.

31

"I'm afraid he's not."

"Have you seen him this evening?"

"I haven't been here for long," said Martin. "I'll inquire, if you like."

"I'd be grateful," said the tall man.

Martin turned, without asking him in; he didn't wait to be asked, but followed Martin into the room. He smiled brightly at the other two, but there was no smile in his eyes, and his gaze was searching. He had a long jaw and a droll mouth, was less good-looking than pleasant of face.

"Have you seen Mr. Clarke to-night, Kathleen?" Martin asked.

"No, not since this morning," said Kathleen. "He was leaving the flat when I took the milk in."

"Oh, I see. Have you been in all day?"

"No, I was out until about half-past six. Then again after eight o'clock."

"Has anyone been here all day?" asked the long-jawed man. His voice remained pleasant and his gaze still searching. "I'm very anxious to have a word with Mr. Clarke."

"Knowing where he was to-day wouldn't help you to have a word with him now, would it?" asked Richard easily.

"Well, no. But he might have given someone an idea of his movements," said the man cheerfully; his gaze seemed almost more searching now that it was turned towards Richard. "Do you live here, gentlemen?"

"Does that matter?" Richard demanded sharply.

Martin smiled.

"No, we came back with Miss Wilder, we live in Leyden Lane. You're Sergeant Wimple, aren't you? Of Scotland Yard?"

The long-jawed man looked surprised.

"Why, yes. How——" He broke off. "*Now* I remember, you're Mr. Fane. There were two brothers, Martin and Richard and—you're Martin Fane. Sons of Jonathan Fane."

"That's right. We met at Scotland Yard, after that miserable business we were mixed up in," Martin said. "Are you a friend of Mr. Clarke?"

His smile took the edge off the question, but didn't alter its significance.

Wimple chuckled.

"Not exactly a friend, I just wanted a word with him. I'll have to try later, or in the morning."

He raised his hand, turned, and went out without another word until he reached the door. "Good night!"

He started down the stairs, and Martin closed the door behind him and turned, to see Kathleen staring up into Richard's eyes, and Richard pursing his lips in a soundless whistle. Kathleen stood up abruptly, went across to the small table, and helped herself to a cigarette. Richard flicked his lighter and held it out to her. As she blew out smoke, he glanced quickly at Martin, and his eyes seemed to say, "Don't scare the wits out of her." He let the lighter cap fall, tossed it into the air, and caught it.

"So the police want him," said Kathleen with a catch in her breath.

"You'd be surprised why they want to see people. He's probably left his car——"

"I don't think he's got a car. Anyway, the police wouldn't call about a trifle at ten o'clock at night—don't be absurd, Richard. Martin, what do you think he wants Clarke for?"

Martin chuckled.

"I'm no good at guessing."

"I wonder if they suspect——"

"Why worry ourselves by wondering about things we know nothing about?"

"Rosa *is* missing. She was worried about Ching— and the way Clarke spoke to me about Ching——" Kathleen actually shivered. "I shan't rest until Rosa's back. Ought we to have told that policeman—what was his name?"

"Wimple."

33

" Told Wimple? "

" Because Rosa has gone out for half an hour and Ching's lost? Nonsense! " Richard went across to the piano and sat on the stool, opened the lid, and began to strum very gently. " Nice tone," he remarked. " You're upsetting yourself over nothing, Kath. I think we might go and see if your deaf neighbour has seen her. After that, just wait until she comes back. I know one thing that would make her rush out—if she had news of Ching."

Kathleen said, " I don't think anything would make Rosa go out without a coat. She's always catching colds, and is afraid of them settling on her chest. It would take a lot for her to go out at all on a night like this, unless she stepped straight into a car."

" I think she'll probably come back soon, and that there will be a simple explanation for it all," Martin said. " I also think it would be silly for you to stay here alone, and you won't want to leave, as Rosa might come back."

Kathleen nodded agreement.

" So you'll have to put up with Richard for a little while," said Martin. " I've one or two things I must do at the flat, and I'm expecting an important telephone call." He wasn't, and Richard knew it, but Richard didn't give him away. " I'll be back soon after eleven, and you'll probably have everything explained by then."

Kathleen nodded again, but obviously didn't believe it.

" It's a shocking risk," Richard said solemnly.

" What's a risk? "

Kathleen turned her head quickly.

" Leaving me here alone with you."

" Idiot," said Kathleen. " Martin, what are you going to do, really? "

" Go back to the flat and get my chores done," said Martin. " Don't worry."

He turned and went out, knowing that both of them were watching him intently. He closed the door and walked firmly to the head of the stairs and down the first flight. The light from the top landing shone right down

34

the well of the staircase, but there were shadowy patches, and he could not be sure that the staircase was as deserted as it appeared to be. He went on down, walking quite normally, until he reached the street door. No one was on the staircase or the landings. He opened the front door cautiously and peered out. He did not think that he could be seen, but saw a man wearing a bowler hat standing some distance along, and just visible in the light of a street-lamp.

He drew back, turned, and tip-toed upstairs. He made no sound, and heard none from Kathleen's flat. As he turned to Clarke's door, he heard the piano; Richard was playing some modern music with a light touch; he was doubtless cheering Kathleen up.

He took out his all-purpose pen-knife. One " blade " was actually a skeleton key, and he had challenged his father to use it. His father had proved that expert knowledge was not necessary.

But for the piano music, he would have felt sure that the sound of metal scraping on metal would be heard in the other flat; it seemed so loud. He didn't take long. The lock went back, and he breathed with relief as he pushed the door open and stepped into darkness. He put the knife in his pocket and closed and locked the door, then shone the torch. This was a different-shaped room from that across the way, and nearly square. It was drably furnished, with neither taste nor quality. Everything looked shabby and the furniture cheap. A heavy blind hung down across the large window. The Axminster carpet was threadbare near the door and near the fireplace, and the piping and tapestry backs and sides of several easy-chairs were worn.

The room was empty.

He went across to the only door which led from here, and found himself in a small passage, with other doors leading off it; two were open, one closed. The first two led to a bathroom and a kitchen; so the bedroom was obviously the room on the other side. He tried the

35

handle, and found that the door was locked. He drew back.

He felt rather like a character in one of his father's books, as he had at the time he had first met Wimple. Then he had discovered that the emotions, while doing something which could be glibly described, were remarkably powerful. He had no right here, had entered on impulse, and had committed burglary. It was possible that the police would come again, and equally possible that Clarke would return home and catch him. If that wasn't enough to put him on edge, there was the mystery of Rosa, the dog, the other woman, and—the closed door.

Why shouldn't a door be locked? He and Richard seldom troubled to lock an inside door at the flat, but his father often locked doors at home. Why not? Why stand there imagining all manner of mystery when the room beyond was almost certainly empty?

He used the skeleton key again; this time he had a much greater feeling of guilt. The notion of starting an unusual kind of business, which had been running through his mind for months, had taken too firm a hold; he was already acting like a private detective—except that he had no real motive.

He opened the door. He did not put on the light immediately, but caught his breath. There was no sound. He held the torch out, shone it, and saw the end of a double bed; no one was in bed. He used his elbow to switch on the light, and found that the room was empty. He was too relieved to feel like laughing at himself. Then he felt absurd; he ought to look under the bed and inside the big mahogany wardrobe. He knelt down; and found nothing. The key was in the lock of the wardrobe door; inside were some clothes, but nothing sinister. Now he felt more normal, and much more like laughing at himself. He went out of the room, switching off the light and using his skeleton key to lock the door from the outside. He had felt convinced, as he believed Kathleen was, that Rosa had come here. Now he could imagine

36

his father, sitting behind a large, square desk, looking up from his typewriter and saying with a faint smile, " In writing this kind of story, Scoop, you get your effect two ways—by rejecting the obvious when the reader expects it to be the answer; and accepting it when the reader is so sure that it's too obvious that it can't be the explanation." The explanation that Rosa had come here was so obvious that he had accepted it too readily.

He had a last look round in the other rooms, and didn't quite know why he troubled to switch on the kitchen light. Even when it was on, shining very bright on the white tiles—this was the brightest room in the flat—he noticed nothing unusual, until his gaze fell on the enamel boiler stove. There was one like it at the flat in Leyden Lane; it heated the water, provided central heating, and burned up rubbish. This had been burning a lot of rubbish lately, because the bottom was choked with white ash. Beside it was a small ash-bucket, half-filled. Something stuck out of the powdery mess.

He went nearer; the " something " was a scorched bone. He stood still, staring as if expecting the bone to move. At last he went and moved his right hand towards a small poker, standing up against the wall. He almost touched it, then snatched his hand away, wrapped a handkerchief round it, lifted the poker and began to stir the bucket's contents cautiously. A faint dust rose, in spite of his caution. He felt little obstructions; the bucket was full of dust, but of harder things too. Bones? The one bone, knuckly at the end which poked out, was quite small—more likely a small animal's than a human being's, Martin thought.

A rabbit's? Or a small dog's? He was still bending over it when he heard a sound outside the flat—a firm footstep. As he straightened up, a key sounded in a lock.

5

MARTIN stepped swiftly to the light switch, looking round desperately. There was no cover in the room; the larder was built above a refrigerator, but there was a shallow recess in a corner behind the door, which opened inwards. Martin closed the door, switched off the light, and slipped into this recess. The man who had entered the flat made little noise, but came straight towards the kitchen-door. He opened it, hiding Martin, put the light on and went to the fireplace. He didn't look round.

He carried a suitcase.

Martin watched him go down on his knees, open the suitcase, and take out a sack; some dust rose from the sack. Slowly and with great care he began to shovel the ashes from the bucket into the sack. When the bucket was empty he opened the front of the boiler stove and scraped more ashes out; several pieces that might have been bone went into the sack. When he had finished, the man put the sack into the case and turned round, keeping his back to Martin most of the time. He had only to glance at the corner to see Martin. Martin was ready to strike, but the man was so anxious to get to the door that he had not closed the case properly. One lock clicked open. He closed it, while holding the case awkwardly, and kept his head turned away.

He was small and round, wore a thick brown overcoat and a bowler hat. Martin glimpsed a dark moustache on a pale face and a scar on the man's right cheek.

The man switched off the light and went out. Martin took two long steps after him, trying to make up his mind what to do. What would his father make a character do? Stop the man now, or wait until he was out of the flat?

Wait, almost certainly; there would be no difficulty in proving that the ashes and bones had come from the boiler here; and if he waited, there would be no danger of being caught out in the burglary. So he stayed by the kitchen-door, until the man opened the front door and stepped through, a hand at the electric-light switch there.

The man cried, " *Oh!* "

" Good evening." It was Wimple's voice. " Is Mr.——"

Martin didn't see what happened, was too anxious to keep out of Wimple's sight. He heard a gasp and a thud. He moved forward swiftly, and caught sight of Wimple reeling back against the landing banisters—and also saw the feet of the little man as he rushed down the stairs, still clutching the suitcase.

Martin kept back. Wimple hit the banisters with a crash—and next moment there was a rending sound, of breaking wood. Wimple toppled backwards, and his feet left the ground. His head disappeared.

Martin thought, " It's broken, he'll fall."

The yawning staircase well was beneath the Yard man, if Wimple fell he would almost certainly break his neck. His right leg was in the air, the tip of his left toe just touched the carpet, one hand gripped a part of the banisters which were still in position.

Another crack made Wimple lurch backwards.

Martin shouted, " Skip! " and rushed forward. One part of the banisters hung over the staircase well, and Wimple seemed doomed to fall. Martin grabbed his right ankle, and leaned back, to take the strain. The jolt as Wimple's full weight fell away from him almost dragged him over. A piece of the banisters fell and crashed below.

Kathleen's door opened, light streamed out, and Richard came hurrying out of the flat.

" What——" he began. He didn't try to finish, paused for a second, then shouted, " Kath get some sheets, tie them together, hurry! " He went down flat on his face,

39

peering over the edge of the little bridge-like landing. " Try and get your other leg up ! " he called, without panic. His own right hand fastened on to Wimple's leg, close to Martin's hand. " I'll take the strain a minute, Scoop, you get yourself comfortable."

Martin was reluctant to let go, but did so. He shifted his position, lay flat, and took hold again. Wimple's right leg was pressing against the side of the landing, with great force; the bone would probably break. Yet if either of them stood too close to the edge, to free the leg, it might give way.

Wimple hadn't lost his head. He managed to move his left leg, and it came in sight. Richard grabbed it. Now they both were lying flat, Martin's feet towards the Clarke's flat, Richard's towards Kathleen's. They could see over the edge, and the strain on their arms was getting worse.

" Hurry ! " called Richard.

There were footsteps in Kathleen's flat, but she didn't appear.

" Why the devil doesn't she hurry ? " growled Richard.

" She's doing her best. All right, Sergeant, we won't let you go. Kath ! "

" Yes ? " Kathleen called from an inner room.

" Stop that, telephone 999, tell them we need firemen here quickly. Must have ladders."

" By the time they arrive——" began Richard.

" Forget it," said Martin. " How are you doing, Wimple ? Can you stand it a bit longer ? "

Wimple's voice floated up, " It looks as if I'll have to."

Then Kathleen's voice came, as she spoke on the telephone. A moment later the bell tinged, and she moved again. Martin felt as if his right arm would break, and Richard wasn't looking too good. Then came a flurry of footsteps, which slackened as Kathleen appeared.

" I've tied two together, will that do ? And a rope, a clothes line."

" Fine," said Martin. " Come forward, step over

Richard—that's right. Now tie a loop in that corner of the sheet, and put it over this foot—leave a good long end, we'll have to tie it again."

Kathleen's hands were unsteady, but she didn't lose much time; and the loop she made seemed a good one. She slid it over Wimple's foot, and tightened it.

" Good. Now take the other end and tie it to the handle of your door, or to something heavy. Better not the handle——"

" Pull a chair towards the door, lay it across so that it can't be pulled through, and tie the rope on to that," said Richard.

" All right." Kathleen disappeared from Richard's sight, but Martin could see her. She pulled the chair into position; there was just sufficient rope to go round one of the legs and to tie, with plenty left at the end for a double knot. She tied that swiftly.

The sheet was now taut.

" I'm going to let you down a bit farther, Sergeant," Martin said. " We won't jerk you. Get ready." He released his grip, but Richard held on while he tugged at the knot round Wimple's foot. " Nice job," he said. " Now ease him downwards, Skip."

Richard did so, until Wimple's feet disappeared. The sheet went over the edge of the landing. Wimple was lowered about a foot from the landing itself, and then the sheets were drawn taut.

Richard got up, slowly. Martin stood up, gulped, shivered, and then looked at the knot tying the two sheets. He smiled into Kathleen's tense face.

" Who taught you to tie knots? "

" Never mind that," snapped Richard.

" I was in the Girls' Brigade," said Kathleen, weakly.

" Girls' Brig——" began Richard explosively.

Martin smiled at Kathleen and went down the stairs. He could see Wimple, hanging head downwards and arms falling; then he switched on the light at the next landing, using his elbow. Wimple was just out of reach of anyone standing on the stairs, there was no way in which they could support him. His face was beetroot red.

"You can't fall now," said Martin reassuringly. " and the fire brigade will be here in two shakes. We'll lower you down, if necessary."

"Your lucky night," Richard said.

Wimple's lips moved.

"Thanks. Telephone the Yard, will you? Information Room—999. Tell them to look for a man who ran from here, brown overcoat, bowler, fibre suitcase about three by two. It's urgent."

"Right."

Martin hurried back upstairs.

"Now that's what I call attention to duty," Richard marvelled. "Scoop, you've a lot to beat. Just take it easy," he added to Wimple, "nothing can go wrong now."

Wimple muttered, "Thanks a million."

As he spoke, police and firemen arrived outside.

· · · · ·

It took three firemen three minutes to lower Wimple to safety. Half an hour after they had arrived, he was sitting in Kathleen's largest easy-chair, drinking a cup of hot, sweet coffee. Martin had pulled up the leg of his trousers and found a nasty wound; he had given first aid expertly, and Wimple stretched the injured leg straight in front of him. He was as pale now as he had been red before, and sweating freely. Kathleen, who had not asked a single question, had made enough coffee for them all, and was in the kitchen, getting more cups, when the front-door bell rang. Martin opened it, and a tall, burly man stood outside, hiding the firemen who were putting up a temporary structure to take the place of the damaged banisters; others were taking the "loose" pieces of the banisters down.

"I believe Sergeant Wimple's here," the man said.

"Yes—come in. From Scotland Yard?"

" Superintendent Kelby," said the burly man.

He was bundled up in an old army greatcoat which was a trifle too small for him, had a ruddy face, rather small blue eyes, and a pleasant manner. He loosened his coat as he came in, and pulled at the flesh which gave him the double chin. He smiled.

" Had a nice time, Jim? "

" I'm all right," muttered Wimple. " Get the chap? "

" We haven't caught anyone yet," said Kelby, " but we've got the suitcase, he ditched it at the end of the road. Too heavy to carry while was running, and he preferred to run."

" Good, that's something," said Wimple. " I'm sorry I fell down on the job."

Kelby chuckled.

" Fell down is about right, from what I've heard. What happened? "

" I saw him go in, and waited for him outside. He walked right into me, but I wasn't prepared for him to kick, and he shot me back against those banisters. Next thing I knew, I was falling backwards. I thought I'd had it." Wimple ran a hand across his wet forehead. " Then Mr. Fane grabbed my foot. He must have been as quick as lightning."

" I was at the door," said Martin truthfully. " Only thing to do. Neither of us lost any time, and I don't know whether we could have held you, if it hadn't been for——"

" The light of the Girls' Brigade," said Richard. " To have your neck saved is something, to have it saved by Kathleen Wilder is *more* than something. What's it all about, Super? The flat across the way been burgled? "

" Looks like it," said Kelby.

" Why keep that up? " asked Richard. " We know Wimple wanted to see Clarke. Was it Clarke, and if so, what's he done? "

" It wasn't Clarke," said Wimple, and he was talking

43

to the Superintendent rather than answering Richard.
" I'd been here, to find out if anyone could tell us where
to find him," Wimple added. "The last they saw of
him was this morning, when the young lady says that she
was getting in the milk as he was leaving."

"When did you last see Mrs. Clarke?" Kelby asked.

Kathleen hesitated.

" They won't bite, and they'll have to know all about
poor Ching," said Richard lightly.

"Well," said Kathleen. " It was the morning before
yesterday. About twelve. She——"

Kelby listened with obviously close attention, Wimple
started to listen, and then leaned back and closed his eyes.
He was still looking very pale. Kelby asked a few
questions, to check times, was very interested in the
account of Clarke's manner to Kathleen, and silent about
the fact that Rosa had disappeared. Martin thought
that he looked very grim.

As Kathleen finished, there was another ring at the
door-bell. A tall, thin, sallow-faced man came in,
carrying a small case; Kelby introduced him as Dr. Hall,
the police surgeon, and Hall gave Wimple one straight
look, and said:

" Let's see that leg."

He did not spend much time on the examination, but
straightened up and said:

" A nasty cut and lacerations—whoever gave first aid
knew his job. It'll do until we get him home."

" Sorry about this," muttered Wimple. " There's
one thing, sir—I got a good look at him. Round, pale-
faced, dark-haired, small dark moustache, a small scar
on the right cheek, just beneath the bone—rather red, and
I'd say fairly recent. He was about five feet six or seven.
And I think I've seen his photo at the Yard."

" Good. We'll check on that," said Kelby. " I'll
send you home now, and I'll call your wife to tell her it's
nothing to worry about."

He went out; and for the first time the others realized

44

that he had more men on the stairs. Two came in, made a chair for Wimple, and lifted him; he could hardly stand on his right leg, which had been badly injured where it had been pressed into the side of the landing.

" Thanks again," he muttered. " One day——"

" Forget it," said Martin.

Wimple shook his head, and was carried out. Kelby saw him as far as the head of the stairs. The firemen were finishing off their first job, and Kelby picked up two pieces of the banisters and examined them closely. He put them down, then returned to the sitting-room of Kathleen's flat. Kathleen was sitting down and looking as pale as Wimple had been. Kelby asked if he could use the telephone, spoke cheerfully to Wimple's wife, then turned to face the others.

" Where is Rosa? " Kathleen demanded. " Where's Mrs. Clarke? What *is* happening? "

" Mrs. Clarke is dead," said Kelby abruptly. He made no attempt to lessen the shock. " We found part of her dismembered body in the river this evening. No doubt that it was murder, either."

KATHLEEN said, " Oh, no," and got up slowly, her gaze on the man from Scotland Yard. " That can't have happened to that poor woman, she——" Kathleen broke off, and looked at Richard. He moved across to her, and took her hand, holding it firmly. " I suppose you know what you're saying. Do you—do you mean that she was killed—over there? "

She nodded towards the front door.

" That's one of the things we'll soon find out," said Kelby. " I'm sorry it's a shock, Miss Wilder. Did you ever hear quarrelling between Mr. and Mrs. Clarke? Or know of anyone who seemed to bear her a grudge? "

Kathleen didn't answer.

" Did you? " Kelby's voice sharpened. " I know it's not pleasant, Miss Wilder, but the quicker we get all the information, the better it will be for everyone."

" I suppose so." Kathleen's face had lost all its colour, and her eyes were dull. That made her look younger; her smallness helped in that, too—it was as if Kelby were talking to a little girl. " No, I can't say that I ever heard them quarrelling, although I know she wasn't happy. Mr. Clarke neglected her so much—he was often away, day and night."

" Do you know where he went? "

" He was a salesman for some firm or other, and always said it was business. Mrs. Clarke didn't seem to doubt that. She was fond of him, I'm quite sure of that."

" Thank you. What about visitors to the flat? "

" They had so few. Now and again she would have someone from St. Peter's—she was a regular churchgoer, although she didn't take any part in the social life of the church. Her husband didn't want her to, he said that he was home so little that he didn't want her gadding about. He could never be sure whether she would be in or out when he did come home."

" Were there any regular visitors? "

" No," said Kathleen.

" How long have you lived opposite, Miss Wilder? "

" Nearly eighteen months."

" And in that time you haven't noticed regular visitors to the Clarkes? "

" No, I haven't. I've told you, they had few visitors. He was almost anti-social—I've only seen him once or twice, and he's never said more than good morning or good evening to me. Mrs. Clarke never talked much, either, it was only when she was alone that she would have a chat. Ching helped her, I know—he was such good company."

" I see. Didn't it strike you as unusual that they should have so few callers? "

" I didn't think about it."

" No reason in the world why you should," said Richard quietly. " Are these questions really necessary, Superintendent? Miss Wilder's had a rough time, and I think she would be happier if you were looking for Rosa Harding—wouldn't you, Kath? "

Kathleen said, " I'm so worried about Rosa."

" Why? " Kelby asked.

Richard told him briefly what had happened.

" We'll do everything we can to find her," Kelby said calmly. " It may not prove anything very serious, you know. I'll want to see you again in the morning, Miss Wilder, and then I may ask you to make a formal statement of what you know of the Clarkes, and when you last saw Mrs. Clarke alive. If I were you, I should get to bed now."

" Bed! As if I could sleep." Kathleen's eyes sparked. " I shan't rest until Rosa's found. If—if he could kill one

47

woman he could kill another. It's so mystifying. Where did Rosa go?"

"We'll find out," said Kelby. "Good night, all."

Martin saw him to the door. The front door of the opposite flat was open, all the lights seemed to be on, and men were moving about. The temporary repair at the landing was finished; it was safe to walk across now. Kelby gave Martin another affable and hearty good night and went into the other flat. Martin closed the door, took out his pipe, and stuck it between his teeth. Richard was standing over Kathleen, who was sitting down again, and saying:

"Of course you won't want to be alone. I'll stay all night, if needs be." The flippant rider, that this would probably ruin her reputation, didn't come; Richard was in an unusually sober mood. Looking at him thoughtfully, Martin decided that it suited him; there were times when he wished that Richard would have sober moods rather more often. "Don't you agree, Scoop?"

He seldom used the old family nickname when anyone else was with them; but he did with Barbara, and had with Kathleen.

Martin rubbed his chin.

"Yes, of course. I don't think that it's wise for you to stay here, though. I think——"

"Don't be a prude."

Martin grinned.

"I was thinking that you might have a lot to do. Mind if I use the telephone, Kathleen?"

She shook her head, and he went across and dialled a number, while Richard looked at him with a crooked smile. Kathleen leaned back and closed her eyes; if appearances were any guide, she had a bad headache. The dialling tone came over the telephone, then it stopped and a woman answered:

"Barbara Marrison here."

"Hello, my sweet," said Martin.

His voice didn't really change, just took on a quality,

48

almost of tenderness, which Kathleen hadn't heard before.

" Scoop! Bless you. I was hoping you'd call before I went to bed. Why *do* I hate days when I can't see you? "

Martin chuckled.

" You can't be normal! " There were moments when he could be as light-hearted as Richard, and he was more often light-hearted with Barbara than with anyone else. " Listen, sweet, I'd like your help. Richard's stumbled into a mystery, and we've both been trying to do something about it—now we need you. Could you pack a toothbrush and everything you'll need for a night, and come over to Buckley Street? To take care of a friend of Richard's."

" Why, yes," said Barbara, without hesitating.

" Fine! Just a moment." Martin put the receiver down and said to Kathleen, " What's the number? "

" Fifty-two."

" Number fifty-two, Flat Number six," said Martin. " You'll be interested, and you'll like Kathleen Wilder, I think—she is Richard's friend! How long will you be? "

" Half an hour."

" Fine," repeated Martin. " 'Bye for now."

He put down the receiver, and found Richard grinning at him.

" The man who knows all the answers is right. This is a good one, Kath. Barbara's his fiancée, and she loves anything with mystery in it. There'll certainly be policemen at the Clarkes' flat all night, nothing can go wrong, and I'll be along bright and early in the morning."

" You're—you're both so good," said Kathleen. " I don't think you ought to have worried your fiancée, Martin. I'd be all right on my own, but—perhaps it's as well. Of course, Rosa might come back any time."

She didn't believe that Rosa would; nor did the others.

. . . . .

49

Exactly half an hour after Martin had finished telephoning, Barbara Marrison arrived. Martin let her in. She was tall for a woman, dark-haired, and with a complexion that rivalled Kathleen's. Her profile was a dream; even Richard admitted it. Her brown eyes could fill with laughter as easily as Richard's, and she had a wholesome quality, as of goodness, which made her liked by most people who met her for the first time. She had worked for years in the investigations department of a large insurance company, usually co-operating with a small private inquiry agency, but for some time now she had been working in a news agency. A year older than Martin, she had a touch of maturity, and at moments could be very grave. Now she was anxious.

" What is it all about, Scoop? "

" Not nice," said Martin. " At least, not all of it's nice, but this part is. This is Kathleen Wilder."

The two young women looked at each other and made appraisal swiftly; Martin judged from the relaxation which followed that they were likely to get on well. He hadn't doubted that when he had sent for Barbara. He motioned to Richard, who told the story briefly, left out nothing of significance, and put in nothing that wasn't needed to give Barbara a complete picture. He had a gift for narration; the whole situation was vivid when he had finished.

By then Barbara was sitting on a low stool near Kathleen, Richard lounging back in an easy-chair, Martin standing and leaning against the mantelpiece.

" Now you know as much as we do," Richard said. " Before we go we'll make sure that there'll be some police about during the night."

" It doesn't matter if there aren't," said Barbara. " We shall be all right. Kath, I think you ought to get to bed, I'll see these two he-men off."

Kathleen, already looking much brighter, stood up, laughed, and said:

" Yes, Captain! Good night, Martin. Thanks for

everything. I didn't realize that it was going to bring you into a mess like this, I just wasn't happy about things. I suppose now that I ought to have told the police right away."

" You did everything anyone could expect."

" That's right." Richard stood in front of her. " And not every one would have had the sense to come to the Fane family with the story. Good night, Kath."

He kissed her lightly on the cheek, and hurried to the door.

Martin kissed Barbara; not on the cheek.

Outside, as the door of Flat 6 closed on them, Martin looked sideways at his brother, and concealed a smile. The signs were unmistakable; Richard was becoming serious about Kathleen, and the speed of events had quickened his realization of it. Richard glanced at him, grinned, and said:

" No sly digs from you! She's a nice girl."

" A very nice girl."

" You don't mean you actually *approve*? "

" Give me time," said Martin.

A police-constable, standing outside the door of Flat 5, which was now closed, was an interested spectator of this little scene; and kept a blank face. He was large, and looked sturdy—an immovable blue pillar of the law. The top of his helmet was on a level with the top of the door.

" Superintendent Kelby gone? " asked Martin.

" No, sir."

" Ask him if he can spare me a few minutes, will you? I'm Martin Fane."

" Just a minute, sir."

The constable rang the bell; it was as sharp and loud as that of the opposite flat. A sergeant answered, the constable talked in a loud whisper, and the sergeant disappeared, only to return almost at once, opening the door wide.

" Come in, Mr. Fane."

51

" Thanks."

Martin went first, and the sergeant raised no objection to Richard following. The living-room was not looking as tidy as when Martin had first come; furniture had been shifted, drawers were open, pictures stood by the side of one wall. More men were in the kitchen than anywhere else. Kelby waved to upright chairs at the far end of the living-room.

" How's Miss Wilder? "

" A friend of ours is staying with her, she'll be all right. Miss Marrison—you probably remember her."

" Oh, yes," said Kelby. His little eyes twinkled. " She is quite an expert on things like this, isn't she? Strange how you've come across another one, Mr. Fane— almost as if you're fated, isn't it? I don't think we'll need your help on this one, though, or your father's."

" Clear case against Clarke? " asked Richard.

" You wouldn't expect me to commit myself yet, would you? No reason why you shouldn't know a little more, though. The devil who did it tried to dismember the body, but the head beat him. He tried to disfigure the face, too—very ugly business, altogether. The body was tied in a sack and dumped into the river near Putney, I should say, but the sack was rotten, the bricks holding it down came out, and—there we were. We had a bit of luck with identification—a bracelet which wouldn't come off easily, and had her name on the inside—the killer probably forgot the name was there, if he ever knew." Kelby paused, and finished, " The rest you know."

" Not everything. What was in the suitcase, and who was the chap who came here? "

" Now that *is* a problem," confessed Kelby owlishly. " The identity, I mean. As for the case—ashes and bones. Part of the body had been burnt—it's never a satisfactory job in a kitchen-stove, though."

" Sure they're human bones? " Martin asked.

" *Quite* sure. If you're thinking of that dog, you needn't run away with the idea that he was killed and the body burnt. Not here, anyhow. Not much point in burning a dog's body, either. It's a grisly business, and I'm afraid it will all come out in the Press. I should try to prepare Miss Wilder for it, if I were you. The man who ran——" He shrugged. " Possibly a friend of Clarke's, if Clarke did the job, but remember we're not sure about that yet. We are sure of one thing, Mr. Fane—if it hadn't been for you and your brother, we should have lost one of the most promising men we have at the Yard. You'll be hearing more about that soon."

" Forget it."

" The Yard *doesn't* forget things like that. I——"

Kelby broke off, for there was a sound outside—of someone running up the stairs. He got up slowly, and the others looked towards the door. The running person drew nearer; the footsteps were light, undoubtedly those of a woman. Suddenly a woman cried out:

" Kath—Kath—Kath! "

" Now I wonder if that could be Miss Rosa Harding," murmured Kelby.

The Fane brothers beat him to the door by a yard.

7

" KATH ! " cried the woman again.

She reached the top of the stairs as Martin and Richard opened the door, and peered over the shoulders of the constable, who was as startled as the others. She was of medium height, wore a tweed suit and a thick woollen scarf round her neck, the ends flying. She had the figure of a Juno—a tiny waist and thrusting bosom. Her eyes were blazing, her colour was high—she wasn't beautiful in the accepted sense, but she was a striking creature. Her movements had the grace of a deer. Perhaps the most astonishing thing was the way she ignored the policeman and the damaged banisters, but swung towards the door of Kathleen's flat, crying:

" *Kath !* "

Hugged close to her breast was a dog; a small, golden-brown Pekinese, who seemed to take it as his right to be hugged just like that.

" *Kath !* " cried the woman.

The door opposite opened, and Kathleen Wilder appeared with Barbara just behind her. Martin couldn't see Kathleen's face, the other woman hid it from him. Richard moved forward, and saw the astounded delight in Kathleen's eyes.

" I've found him ! " cried Rosa. " He's all right, he isn't hurt, oh, isn't it *won*derful ! "

She raised Ching high above her head, resting him on her palms, as if she were offering a sacrifice to an unseen God. Ching, looking supremely disinterested, decided to sneeze.

" Darling, I'm so overjoyed, you wouldn't believe," cried Rosa Harding. " Just look at him. His coat needs a comb, poor dear, and I'm sure he's hungry, although they said he wouldn't eat anything. I don't suppose they offered him the right food, do you? Poor *sweet*, he must have been terrified. It was all so funny, too, I was told——"

She broke off, as if seeing Barbara for the first time. Then she laughed. It was one of the most astonishing things that the Fane brothers had ever heard, because with the laugh she changed completely. One moment, she was a semi-hysterical woman, behaving like a fool over a dog; the next, she laughed on a low-pitched note, as if really amused; and she was no longer even slightly excited.

" My dear, I'm *so* sorry. I didn't know you had a friend in. Aren't I being absurd over a dog? " She didn't put Ching down, but hugged him closer. " I don't think we've met, have we? "

Kathleen said, " It's Barbara Marrison, I—— Rosa, you frightened the wits out of me! "

" Frightened you, dear? How? "

" You told Martin Fane something amazing had happened."

" Well, it *had*," said Rosa. " I had a telephone call from Fifi, you know how Fifi always *loved* Ching. She said she was passing a pet shop this afternoon and was *sure* she saw Ching in the window. In a cage. Wasn't it *dreadful*? It was over in Lambeth Road. She telephoned, but we were out, and she telephoned again this evening. I rang you, I was so excited, and then I thought I heard Ching bark, I hardly knew what I was doing. I rushed out, got a taxi, and went right to the shop. Luckily the people who own it live in the flat above, and they let me see the dogs, and it *was* Ching. They say they found him wandering about, but I can't believe it, they're nothing but dog thieves. I didn't want to make a fuss, though, so I paid them four guineas for him. He's worth fifty! I'll never be able to thank Fifi enough."

" Good—Lord! " said Richard faintly.

Rosa appeared to realize that someone was standing behind her, and on that whispered comment she looked over her shoulder. She frowned; but even then Martin could not fail to notice the arresting lines of her face and its striking handsomeness. It was almost unbelievable that a woman who could look like that would make a fool of herself over a dog.

Kathleen stepped forward, and spoke in a smothered voice.

"Rosa, this is Martin Fane. You know Richard, don't you? And this is Barbara—oh, I told you. Richard and Martin came over with me, and you were gone. I was worried, in case something had happened to you."

"But *darling*, what could have happened to me?"

Kathleen, her eyes sparking dangerously and her fists suddenly clenching, drew in a sharp breath, and cried:

"Well, you could have been murdered!"

"Don't be silly, dear."

"Don't be silly! Of all the idiocy, running out without leaving any message! Ching was only in a *shop*. He wasn't being neglected, obviously he must have been well looked after, or they wouldn't have kept him in the shop window for everyone to see. You must be mad! You've made a fool of that dog, you couldn't fuss him more if he were a baby. And look at him. Look!" She pointed a quivering finger at Ching, whose wrinkled nose seemed to be turned up disdainfully, and whose furry coat fell over Rosa's arms, his tail hanging down by her hip. "*Look* at him. Fat, smug, spoiled, pampered—you ought to be shot!"

Throughout all this Rosa stared with her mouth slightly open, as if she couldn't believe her ears. Barbara kept a straight face. Richard had difficulty in hiding a grin. Martin watched the animated face of the smaller woman approvingly.

"Well!" breathed Rosa. "You must be out of your senses. We've been so worried——"

"*You've* been worried!"

56

" I always understood that you were attached to Ching," said Rosa coldly. " I quite understand, in future, that you can't really be trusted to take care of him. Mrs. *Clarke* will be more kind, and——"

" Mrs. Clarke's dead. *Murdered!* "

Rosa drew back a pace; Martin shifted his toe quickly, to get away from her heel. Silence fell upon the room, like a heavy pall.

" No," Rosa breathed.

" She is. The police have been here. We've had a terrible time. Look at the banisters. Can't you see the policeman? It's been dreadful—really dreadful. And you were gadding about looking for that pampered bit of fluff."

" Kath, please," said Rosa in a shaky voice. " I'd no idea. It's terrible. Poor Mrs. Clarke. Who——"

She broke off.

Tears were glistening in Kathleen's eyes.

" Oh, you poor dear," said Rosa, " now I can understand how you feel. I'm awfully sorry, Kath, I am really. Ching, go into the kitchen, you'll find some milk there." She put the dog down, almost roughly, and approached Kath, hand outstretched. " Forgive me, dear."

Kathleen was now crying openly.

Barbara waved her hand at the Fanes, shooing them away. They went.

.   .   .   .   .

" Nice spirit, our Kathleen," said Richard as they stepped into the street. " Brrrh, it's cold! " He glanced at a policeman standing on duty outside. " Funny thing, now—but Martin. My hat, what a couple of Fleet Street men! I'm worse than you. I'm a journalist, remember. A *journalist*, and I've missed the biggest scoop this year. Good Lord! " He stood by the side of the Buick, looking ludicrously crestfallen. " No wonder I've no future on Fleet Street. Neither of us. It's—fantastic. What on earth's got into me? "

57

" Young love," said Martin dryly.

" No, hang it, not a time for joking."

" It's a time for truth. Nip upstairs, Skip, and ask Kelby if the Press has the story yet. No one's about, and you may still be in time."

" Right. Won't be a jiff."

Richard turned towards the house, and Martin walked briskly into the wind. He already felt cold, and slipped his hands into his pockets. He wondered which way the little man had run when he had finished with Wimple. Towards the Strand, almost certainly—he was now walking away from the Strand, towards the river. The wind came off there like a knife.

Kelby knew all about the ashes, and had a description of the man who had escaped from the flat—a better one than he could have given if he had admitted breaking in. There was no point now in making an admission. The whole grisly business looked as if it were over, as far as he was concerned. With Rosa missing, Richard would have insisted on going on with it, but there was no point in insisting now. Richard might well decide that it was foolish to go on, as it would upset Kathleen. As a problem, it didn't seem to offer much; Clarke was obviously the murderer, and——

Was he?

If so, why had someone else come to clear the ashes out of the grate? Why hadn't Clarke come himself? If Clarke had been the only man concerned, he wouldn't have employed anyone else to come and collect the evidence; that would have been playing into the man's hands. He went over several recent murder cases; in every one the murderer had kept everything to himself, had confided in no one—had had no one's help. Murder was a lonely business, but Wimple, talking out of turn because he was not feeling so good, had made it clear that the man had not been Clarke.

Richard came hurrying back, and shouted cheerfully:

" Kelby's seen no news hounds. There may have been

58

some at the Back Room at the Yard, but he hasn't heard about it. I think I'll go along and see Danny Lee at the World Agency. He'll spread it as far as anyone. Unless you think a single paper would pay better."

" It wouldn't get round so much."

" We'll do a special article and sign it between us," said Richard.

" No, you sign it."

Richard chuckled.

" Certainly not, an even split in credit and in cash for this." He sat at the wheel of the Buick and started off. " Hold your head, I'm going fast, or the telephone wires will start buzzing."

He raced the car towards the end of the street, while Martin looked at him thoughtfully; and affectionately. There was a spontaneous generosity in Richard which overcame many of his shortcomings. The simple truth was that he hadn't yet found the right niche or the right woman. It looked as if he might be half-way towards the right woman, but——

" Scoop! " Richard shouted, as he swung into the Strand and made several pedestrians look at him.

" Careful."

"Scoop, listen. Were you serious about your proposition to-night? "

" I was."

" Cross your heart and all that? "

Martin gave him a crooked smile.

" Yes. What's got into you? "

" Listen," said Richard, taking his eyes off the road, and earning a curse from a taxi-driver coming in the opposite direction. " The business is on. It started yesterday. Well, this morning. We want a name for it, and we want it quick. Lame Dog's no use, it'll get us too many laughs. See what I'm driving at? "

He swung round a huge red bus, into Aldwych.

Martin said, " Yes, I think I do."

His eyes were glowing.

59

"My dear chap, we ought to have seen it hours ago. Certainly from the moment Kelby said murder. Look at what's been handed us on a plate. Fane brothers scent mystery. Story of missing dog led to unearthing of dastardly murder. It didn't, but that's by the way, the story's worth plenty. There's more—heroic rescue of Scotland Yard man, we can use that. Our first case, and we can sell it to the World Agency and get more publicity to-morrow than we could buy for a fortune. We can't miss it."

"We won't miss it," Martin said softly.

"Name, name, give us a name," pleaded Richard.

He slowed down as they passed the Law Courts and entered Fleet Street, where it narrowed towards the City and, nearer at hand, the offices of many of the national newspapers. Lights were glowing at some windows, but there was little traffic. A few men strolled along, and they passed a narrow turning in which two men were standing and singing, softly, one acting as conductor; nearby was one of the inns of Fleet Street, where journalists foregathered and the failures or the foolish got drunk.

"The *name*," breathed Richard. "Fane Brothers. Don't say it's cashing in on the Maestro, he won't mind."

Martin said, "You've got it. While you're talking to Danny Lee, I'll telephone Dad. He won't be in bed yet. He'll probably think up a name, just like that, and we could get his blessing, too. If we do need a bit of extra capital that'll be useful. You'll have to borrow your two-fifty from him, won't you?"

"Most of it."

"I'll talk to him," said Martin.

Richard pulled up outside a tall, grimy building, where there were lights at all the upper-floor windows but none at ground level. He hurried ahead of Martin. The World News Agency was on the second and third floors here, and there were plenty of telephones in the outer office. Richard had disappeared into some inner sanctum before Martin went into a telephone booth; one with a

60

pay-in-advance coin box. He had no change, so put in the call to Lichen Abbas 33 and asked the operator to reverse the charges. He smiled faintly as he did that; when his father took the call he would assume that only Richard would be without funds.

It looked a golden chance, but he was a little uncertain how his father would take it. His mother would most certainly disapprove. He smiled more broadly; she would soon come round.

" Well, Richard? " came Jonathan Fane's voice over the telephone.

8

JONATHAN FANE sat back in the chair at his desk, in the study of his Dorset home—Nairn Lodge, Lichen Abbas, He moved his glasses slightly, stretched out a hand for a cigarette, without quite realizing what he was doing, lit it, and then flipped over the page of a typewritten manuscript in front of him. Superimposed were alterations in red and green ink ; he was giving a story its final revision. A sheaf of notes, from his readers, was next to the manuscript, and he was weighing up the merits and demerits of a criticism.

It was nearly eleven o'clock.

He started violently when his door opened.

" Darling, aren't you *ever* coming to bed to-night? " Evelyn Fane, in a royal blue dressing-gown, came sweeping into the book-lined study. She was frowning, and that made a little vertical groove appear between her eyes. " *Must* you work every minute there is? "

" Eh? "

" Don't pretend you didn't hear me. It's past eleven."

" It's not, it's only just turned five to," said Jonathan Fane defensively.

" Your clock must be slow. Darling, you'll overdo it, you know." Evelyn came up to the desk, sat on the corner and on a page of the manuscript, and looked into her husband's grey eyes. " It isn't as if it mattered, I'll bet that book won't be published for two years."

" Eighteen months," corrected Jonathan mildly. " It's the new Prince yarn. I was just on the last page or two of a chapter."

" Isn't it remarkable how you always reach the last page or two of a chapter about three hours too late? All

62

the time I've known you, you've lived in the study. Every excuse you could ever find for doing more work, you found. You'll make yourself ill, and it's not as if you need to now. Look at your eyes! They're watering, and——"

" It's the smoke."

" You smoke too many cigarettes, too. Why don't you smoke a pipe when you're reading? You've been saying you would for twenty years."

" Sorry, dear," said Jonathan, and gave a little quirk of a smile; his eyes were twinkling. " I won't be five minutes. Go and get the bed warm."

" I will not. I'm going to stay here and wait until you come," said Evelyn.

Fane's eyes twinkled more brightly.

" Oh, you fool," she said, and suddenly bent down and kissed him. " Don't overdo it, sweet. You seem to think you can work as hard now as you could twenty years ago. I know we had that month on the Riviera, but you were always longing to get to the typewriter, even then. Make do with me, for a change."

" Thank you, dear."

" Idiot! " Evelyn stood up, tall, with grey hair parted in the middle. Her grey-green eyes were youthful, when she smiled her teeth showed, very white. She was thin, almost too thin; and for a woman in the middle fifties, remarkably attractive and well preserved. Her hands, long, white, and shapely, moved to his face. " Darling, you've turned sixty, remember."

" As if I could forget, when I'm reminded every day," Fane stood up and laughed. He was the same height as his wife, big and burly, plump but not really fat. Although it was not warm in the big study, he wore a cream-coloured linen coat and a pale-blue shirt without a tie. Cigarette-ash littered the big, smooth desk. His iron-grey hair grew well back on his forehead, and waved a little. Full face, he was good-looking, but he needed a bigger chin for his profile, and there was a little bag of flesh

63

beneath what chin there was. " All right, I surrender, I'll finish that in the morning. It's a pity, really."

" No, it isn't."

" It is. I wanted to get that chapter finished before going away for the week-end, and I can do it by eleven in the morning. I never like getting to London much after lunch, it doesn't give me time to go and see Matthew. He's booked us for the new show at the Apollo, by the way. Nice and emotional, I'm told, every woman's joy."

" Darling! You didn't tell me that——"

" Half the fun's spoiled if you know in advance. I've kept the week-end free from social obligations here. We can spend a few hours with the boys—I expect they'll be in town for the week-end, you can spend Saturday morning window-shopping. Window, remember! "

Evelyn stood up, went to a large hide arm-chair, and sat down.

" I've never known anyone to get his own way so easily," she said helplessly. "You can work until half-past eleven, not a minute longer, and I'm going to sit here while you do it. Darling, it's a delightful surprise. I want to see the boys, and——"

She broke off abruptly, and gazed at him intently.

" Now what? " asked Fane.

" Why *do* you want to go to London? "

" Just to take a week-end off. If I'm here I'm always in the study."

" No other reason? "

" None at all."

" I wonder," said Evelyn, and laughed. " I'll soon find out. I expect Matthew wants to see you about something—new contracts, or that Swiss business. Don't think you're going to Switzerland without me, darling, will you? "

" I wouldn't dream of it."

" You might dream of it," said Evelyn, " but that's as far as you'll go."

Fane chuckled—and the telephone bell rang. As he

stretched out his hand for it, his wife frowned again, and looked anxious. She was framed by one of the bookcases, in which Fane kept his Prince stories—easily his best-selling books.

" I wonder who wants us as late as this ? " Evelyn asked.

" It's almost certainly terrible news from London," Fane said dryly. " Richard's probably been thrown out of a night-club. Hallo ? . . . Oh, yes, I'll take it." He grinned up at his wife. " A Mr. Fane speaking from a call-box in London would like me to accept the charge for the call, so that's Richard, and he probably doesn't want Martin to hear what he's saying. And *that*——"

" Means money," said Evelyn slowly.

" Probably. He's been very good lately, but——"

" Darling, you're too soft with him."

" Am I ? "

" Yes, and I'm worried about him. His job, I mean. I don't like to think he's writing a gossip column. He seems unsettled, and——"

" Here he is," said Fane, and his voice became very deep. " Well, Richard ? "

He listened; and chuckled.

" Yes, you caught me out that time, Scoop. . . . No, we aren't in bed yet, although we should have been if your mother had had her way." He smiled across at his wife. " What's that ? . . . *What's* that ? "

He listened intently. Evelyn knew that it was something of importance but nothing to worry about, and relaxed in her chair as she watched him. Except for the iron-grey hair and a few lines at his eyes and forehead, he looked exactly the same as he had twenty years ago. The almost youthful enthusiasm, which had been surprising at forty, was more remarkable now. He was a slave to his own work, a slave to anyone who could persuade him to work for them. For years she had been afraid that he would push himself to a collapse, but he seemed to be able to withstand the pressure and the concentration as easily as ever. Now she could tell that he was concentrating, from the way he kept pressing his lips together and moving them slightly; by the quick "Yes, I see," which he kept saying. He didn't smile, but she judged from his expression that he was pleased.

"I *see*," he said at last. "Well, yes. I think it might be a good notion. It's worth trying, anyhow. Yes, I'll do that . . . ten per cent of the profits in return!" He chuckled. "I know, I'm a hard-headed business type. . . . Eh? . . . I don't know about a name. . . . Hold on a minute." He put his hand over the mouthpiece, and smiled into his wife's face. "They're going to start a kind of private inquiry agency, and want a name for it in a hurry. Can you think of one?"

"*What?*" Evelyn sat up abruptly.

"Good idea, too, and solves your worry about——"

"A detective agency? You mean—Jon, what on earth are you saying? Give me that telephone. It's utter nonsense. *Inquiry* agents! We have quite enough crime in this family, and Scoop—do you mean Scoop has actually let Richard talk him into a hare-brained scheme like that?"

Fane grinned.

"Hold on, Scoop, your mother wants a word with you—and hold your breath."

He handed over the telephone, and his wife clapped it to her ear and began to tell Martin what she thought of him, of the suggestion, and of everyone who had anything to do with it.

Fane picked up a pencil, held it poised over a pad of pink-tinted paper, then began to scribble. He started with *Lamedog*, went on to *Fane Brothers*, and put other names beneath each, in two columns. "*Gaydog, Gayley, Gaydon, Lame Dog—Fane Agency, Famous, Fame.*" He didn't like any of them. He glanced up at his wife; Martin was doing well, for she was listening. Beyond her, he could see the large bookcases, almost filled now with his books; he had not been called an industrious fantast for nothing. The smallest held the Prince series; stories of a mildly

66

aristocratic private investigator who, for nearly seventy books, had suffered practically every form of danger and conceived every bright and improbable idea anyone could imagine; and most of these several times.

His eyes gleamed, and he stretched up his hand.

" No, I don't agree," said his wife, but there was less emphasis in her voice. " I know Richard's not in the right job, but I can't see—*don't keep pulling at my arm*—I was talking to your father—*Jon, don't*—it's all very well, but you'll only find yourself having to collect evidence for divorce and that kind of unsavoury business, or—*Jon!* "

Fane stood up, kissed her nose, and took the receiver away.

" Scoop, listen, the name's ready made. Prince. It will tie up with the Prince. You'll get a lot of incidental publicity, and so will the Prince. We ought to be able to buy your mother a new hat every month, on the strength of it. Yes, of course I'm sure . . . I shouldn't worry too much about that."

" If you're telling him not to worry about me," Evelyn whispered fiercely, " you needn't waste your breath."

Fane wagged a finger at her.

" No, I shouldn't tag on Agency or Bureau or anything like that, just use the name itself, with a kind of slogan— Prince will solve your troubles, or something like that. You needn't fix that to-night, but you can put the name over all right. . . . Oh, yes, you were right to go to the *World*, this is a big story, and Danny Lee will look after you. Give him my regards, and good luck. Oh, we'll be up to-morrow, anyhow, and——"

" Jon! I want to speak! " cried Evelyn.

" Your mother sends her love," said Fane, and dropped the receiver back into the cradle. He leaned back in his chair and looked at her, his eyes gleaming, his lips parted in a smile which curved the corners of his lips. " My sweet, I don't know how you manage to wear so well."

Evelyn drew in a deep breath, and stormed:

" It isn't because I have to live with *you*. You're

67

enough to put ten years on my age. You not only condone nonsense like this, you let them use the Prince. Why, it— it's the craziest thing you've ever done, and you've done some crazy things. People will think *you're* mixed up in it——"

" I am. I'm putting up five hundred pounds."

" What! " breathed Evelyn.

" And I've told him I want ten per cent of the profits," said Fane urbanely.

" Profits? There won't be any profits, it'll all be lost and——"

" Then we'll be able to set it off against income tax, so it won't really be a big loss."

"Whenever you want to go in for some silly extravagance you talk about setting it off against income tax," said Evelyn hotly. " I haven't been so sure about that for a long time, you think it's easy to get past me with it, but I doubt if you claim it. You'd say it wasn't fair or legal or something. I——"

She caught her breath.

" Listen, darling," said Fane, " they've stumbled into a murder case—no, no danger to them!—and they'll be in all the newspapers to-morrow morning. So will the Prince. We'll find that before long people will begin to think that the Prince is a real person, it's the one thing we needed to make him go farther. He's been selling at the same rate for two or three years, and we wanted another boost. This will boost both the Prince and the boys. It's the best publicity notion I've had for years."

" You and publicity! *And* your notions, half of them come to nothing."

" Now and again they come off," said Fane urbanely. " Let's get to bed, my sweet. We can go and see what they're up to, to-morrow—no, I did *not* know this was in the offing when I planned the week-end." He slid his arm round her waist, and led her towards the door; she held herself rigid. " I think you'll be glad about this, before it's over. Martin's going ahead fast, he says he knows of some offices they can take over first thing in the morning, he'll paint the sign on the door himself, and they'll be ready for customers. Barbara's in it, by the way, and—great Scott, I forgot!"

" Not something else," said Evelyn in alarm.

" Well—I don't know how serious it is. Richard seems to have found a girl at last. According to Martin, she——"

" Richard a *girl*? This gets worse and worse. Who is she? Do we know her? Oh, Jon, you fool, that's far more important than anything else." Evelyn was aghast. " You don't know what he might get himself mixed up in. Richard—I've dreaded the day when I'd hear that. Barbara's all right, we were lucky with Scoop, but *Richard*. We must see her soon."

" Isn't that arranged?" asked Fane. " To-morrow, maybe."

She strained away from him, looked into his eyes, began to smile, and then yielded against him.

9

MARTIN, always the early riser, woke just after seven o'clock next morning, and blinked up at the ceiling. One room at the flat had been divided by a wooden partition to make two small bedrooms; there was only just room for a dressing-table and a tall-boy in each, besides a bed. They shared a large wardrobe in a passage leading from the head of the stairs to the kitchen. They could hear the traffic, as lorries and vans left Covent Garden Market, not far away, laden with vegetables and flowers for the suburban shops and markets. One lorry rumbled beneath the window so loudly that Martin marvelled that Richard could sleep through it. Richard had learned to sleep through anything.

Martin got out of bed, stretched up, yawned, and rubbed his eyes; and all the time he was smiling. He recalled everything he had said to his father and everything his father had said to him. He had hoped for approval, but not expected enthusiasm; he ought to have known better. He went along to the front door, pulled the papers out of the letter-box, then went into the kitchen and put on a kettle. He was reluctant to open the folded newspapers; his hopes were so high and might be dashed. Danny Lee had promised Richard that they would have a good show, but that was really in the hands of the individual newspapers to whom the Agency sold the story. It might have been wiser, after all, to have concentrated on one newspaper; none had less than a million circulation, most had several millions, and the publicity in any one would have been worth a fortune.

He opened the *Daily Record*. His eyes shone when he saw the headline, front-page edge.

JON FANE'S SONS
SAVE YARD MAN

He read on:

A Scotland Yard detective sergeant, brutally attacked at a flat in the Adelphi last night, was saved from falling over broken banisters to his death by Martin and Richard Fane, sons of Jonathan Fane, famed crime writer. Scotland Yard was prompt to acknowledge its debt to the Fane brothers, who were making private investigations into the death of Emma Maude Clarke, part of whose dismembered body was found in the Thames last evening.

This was their first investigation since the formation of a private inquiry agency, known as " Prince ". The Prince is the hero of . . .

" Perfect! " Martin breathed.

All the other papers named them and Prince; several gave them headlines. He put the papers on the kitchen-table, and chuckled aloud. The chuckle was accompanied by a bubbling sound from the kettle; it was boiling, and he hadn't noticed it. He turned the gas low, and it went out with a pop. He laughed aloud, lit the gas again, and was putting the tea in the warmed pot when a tousled head appeared at the door.

" Can't a man sleep? " Richard said complainingly.

" Who wants to sleep? Come and look at these, if you can rub the sleep out of your eyes? "

" Go easy."

Richard yawned, and appeared in a pair of pyjamas, pale blue in colour, and cut so well that he looked almost dressed; his lean figure lent itself to clothes of all kinds. He whistled when he saw the first paper, and began to laugh. Martin was grinning broadly as he made the tea. They sat at each side of the kitchen-table, sipping, reading, beaming at each other in delight.

The clock in the living-room struck the half-hour.

" We've plenty to do," said Martin. " I took a chance when I said we were at Quill Chambers. If we can't get those offices we'll have to turn the flat into an office. What time does Paddy Smith usually get up? "

" Don't ask me."

" Better not try him before eight o'clock," Martin reflected. " If he says it's all right we'll need furniture. I think we'd better hope for the best, and you'd better go furniture hunting, and get the stuff ready for delivery. It's a bit too quick, really, but we may just pull through."

" We'll get through," said Richard. " As I have to be out early, you cook breakfast, I'll shave."

Martin cooked breakfast five mornings out of seven, for a variety of reasons always advanced by Richard. He cooked a large one. They were sitting down to it at the kitchen-table when the telephone bell rang. Richard waved to the door, and Martin went out of the little kitchen.

" Martin Fane," said Martin, and expected to hear a newspaper man.

" Good morning, *Prince*, darling."

" Barbara! Hallo! This is wonderful! What are you doing up so early? "

" I couldn't sleep, I had a feeling that there'd be something worth waking up for. I've read the papers. Darling, it's superb, but what will the Maestro say? "

" It was his idea."

" Well, well," said Barbara, and Martin could hear the laughter in her voice. " I'll bet your mother will have a word to say to him about this."

" She'll be all right when she's got used to the idea," said Martin confidently. " I've never known her let us down yet. How are *you*? "

" Fine."

" Everybody? "

" Kathleen's just woken up. Rosa's still sleeping, with Ching by her side. They put up a camp bed for me —I thought I'd stay. Kathleen was nervous, and I didn't

72

think that Rosa would be much help to her. Rosa's somewhat masterful, isn't she? "

" I don't know her."

" You've seen her once, and that ought to be enough. I'm going to leave after a snack here. Is there anything I can do? "

Martin talked. . . .

Bacon and eggs were cold on his plate when he returned. Richard had already finished, and was looking spruce and attractive. He was reading the *Record* story again, and still enjoying it, but he glanced up quickly.

" How's Kath? "

" Only just awake, she had a good night."

" Thank the Lord for that."

" Really serious, Skip? " asked Martin lightly.

" It wouldn't surprise me."

" I see. Mum and Dad are coming up this morning. It was laid on, I gather—astonishing how he always seems to fix a London trip for the right day, isn't it? I mentioned Kathleen to him last night, so be prepared for an inquisition."

Richard looked down his nose; but soon smiled.

.   .   .   .   .

Paddy Smith, the energetic senior partner of the firm which managed the block of offices known as Quill House, Strand, London, W.C.2, was also a friend of Martin's. He was up when Martin telephoned, just before eight o'clock. He was sympathetic and helpful. It would take some fixing, it might only be a temporary let, but yes, they could move into the suite of three offices this morning. He would telephone the caretakers and fix that.

Richard was leaning over his chair as Martin talked.

" All set? "

He was eager.

" Off you go. Barbara will be at the office at nine, we'll expect the furniture at the door by half-past and the doors open by ten," said Martin.

" Paint my name on the door nicely, won't you? "
Richard waved, and hurried out. He stopped at the
front door, and called, " Oh, Scoop."

" Yes? "

" All right for me to take the car? I'll have to do more
dodging about, and may even get some stuff in the car
itself. Of course, if you'd rather have it——"

" Don't crash it," said Martin.

Richard said, " Thanks, old chap," and hurried out.

The door slammed, to cut off his cheerful whistle.
Martin, shaved but not dressed, went thoughtfully into
the bathroom, his spirits high.

.   .   .   .   .

The name, just the word PRINCE, was on the outer door
of the three offices, black against the frosted glass panel.
That was at five minutes to ten. Inside, three removal
men in shirt-sleeves were labouring to put desks and
chairs in the right places; there had been no time to get
carpets or floor covering. Cabinets were against the
walls, two suitcases filled with papers from the flat were
on the floor, and Martin and Barbara were preparing to
put some on the desks and give the impression of great
activity. There were two typewriters; Barbara's portable
and a second-hand standard Underwood. Barbara was
flushed and her hair was untidy, she kept blowing strands
back from her nose. The removal men finished; Martin
nodded with satisfaction, tipped them handsomely, and
showed them to the door. Richard was out; they knew
it was practically impossible to have a telephone number
allotted that day, although there were telephones in the
offices, which had only been vacated a week before.
Richard was attempting the impossible; but if anyone
could persuade the G.P.O. to move quickly, he could.

Martin locked the door.

" Why? " asked Barbara, looking up.

" To make sure we have a few minutes' peace," said
Martin. " I know we're not likely to get many callers,

74

but who knows? Feel like being serious for a minute? "
Barbara took her powder compact and lipstick from a
leather handbag.
" Yes, sweet. What about? "
" We're off to a good start. If we look like making a
success of it six months from now, I'll carry on and hope
for the best."
" It will be a success," Barbara said confidently.
" And six months from now," said Martin, going
over and taking the lipstick out of her hand, " we shall get
married. To the day. It's Friday the 14th of March.
On the 14th of September——"
Barbara's eyes were glistening.
" Yes, my darling."
" Come what may? "
" Come what may, success or failure."
He crushed her to him; and when she moved back, a
minute later, her eyes were shining; and there was red
on his lips. She took a red handkerchief from her handbag and handed it to him. He watched every movement
she made, and marvelled at what he knew to be his great
good fortune. There was—there could be—only one
Barbara. The eager vitality of her expression, the beauty
of her chestnut-coloured eyes, the swift, sure movements
of her hands, all fascinated him.
She was putting on lipstick when there was a sharp tap
at the outer door.
" Customer! " whispered Barbara. " Hurry."

.   .   .   .   .

It was not a customer; it was Superintendent Kelby,
who came bustling in, glanced round, nodded con-
gratulation, and said with his tongue in his cheek that he
expected to co-operate a great deal. He wanted to ask
several questions about the incidents of last night, none
of them serious. As he went out, a middle-aged man with
a drab-looking face and drooping moustache sidled into
the room. They hardly noticed him at first, and he stood

75

meekly just inside the room, until Barbara realized he was there and hurried across to him.

" Good morning."

" 'Morning," said the little man sadly. " You are the people who find things, aren't you? "

" We find a great number of things." Barbara kept a straight face, but Martin had to turn his back and appear busy at a filing-cabinet. He could have gone into one of the two smaller offices which led off this, but didn't want to miss a word. " Have you lost something? "

" Yes, I have," said the little man miserably. " I've tried the police, and they don't seem able to do anything. I've tried the insurance company, and *they* aren't interested. Not much, anyhow, and it's worth fifty quid. My watch," he explained unhappily. " It's a gold one, a present from my wife ten years after we were married. I wouldn't mind so much, if it wasn't from her, she died last year, and somehow——" His voice went on and on, miserably. " It doesn't mean much to anyone else, it means a lot to me. I lorst it last Friday. I'd pay a fiver to anyone who could find it for me. On a bus. It *must* have been on the bus, I looked at it before I left the Rose and Crown, and I hadn't got it when I reached home. So it must have been on the bus. The Lorst Property Orfice haven't found it, but it must have been on the bus. Think you can do anything? "

" We'll try," said Barbara briskly.

" Mind you, payment by results. I don't want to pay a fee and then——"

" We only charge on results, Mr.——"

" My name's Kennedy, Charlie Kennedy. Okay, then."

" Come and sit down, Mr. Kennedy, and I'll make some notes," said Barbara, still briskly.

Martin had given up trying to keep a poker face, and was in one of the two rooms that led off the large main one. There was a counter near the front door, and a room to the right and to the left. His was on the left; he would share it with Barbara, but she was in the outer smaller room now. In his the window overlooked the wall of another building; the outlook could not have been much more drab; nor could their first customer. The chances of finding the watch were negligible, but there was a sentimental motive, and they would do their damnedest. There was a touch of unreality about the venture—there probably always would be. There was the unreality of a dream about the promise for the 14th of September, too. He found himself smiling.

The office bell rang again, and he went to answer it. Barbara was still listening to Charlie Kennedy's droning story. Another man had come into the office, small, ill-dressed, ill-favoured; certainly not a customer. Martin went across and smiled as if the other were dressed like a millionaire.

" Good morning! "

" 'Morning." The man glanced over his shoulder, as if nervously, drew closer to Martin, and lowered his hoarse voice. " Must speak to you, it's urgent. That Clarke job. You're on it, aren't you? "

10

MARTIN looked into the man's eyes; small, dark, hard eyes; but steady. He took stock of the visitor thoroughly for the first time. The man had a small face, and hadn't shaved for several days; his stubble was grey and black. There was a bare patch beneath his lower lip, where the hair didn't grow properly. His lips were thin, and there was yellowish matter at the corners, and sleep in his eyes. His nose was broken, and looked snub. He had a sloping forehead, and his dark hair, shot with grey, grew low. It was overlong; a tweed cap pressed over his head made hair bulge out beneath it. He wore an old, black patched overcoat, his dirty collar and bright tie were both frayed. His voice was hoarse, as if he were suffering from a severe cold, but nothing else suggested that.

" Well? Are you on it or ain'tcha ? "

" Come with me," said Martin. He turned towards his office, but the outer door opened again. A middle-aged woman stepped in. Martin swung round and beamed. " I won't keep you two minutes, madam." He went into his own small office, told the man to sit down, scribbled a note to Barbara, and went into her with it. The man with the bedraggled moustache was talking drably on. Martin handed Barbara the note, and went out as she read:

> " *A bite on the C. case. Get the office empty and lock the door.*"

He closed his own door. His visitor, who hadn't taken off his cap, was now sitting in an arm-chair, with padded seat and arms, which had been in a shop window an hour

78

before. Martin went to his desk, which had been in the basement of the same shop, and offered cigarettes.

" Ta."

Martin flicked his lighter.

" So you know something about the Clarke job, do you? "

" That's right, guv'nor."

" Seen the police? "

" Nark it. What do you fink I've come 'ere for? "

Martin smiled; and his mother would have been astonished, for she would have found that it was a nasty smile.

" For a rake-off," he said.

The eyes, so small and dark, had a certain directness; the man actually grinned. There was nothing likeable about him, yet that was disarming.

" S'right," he said. " Not that I would go to the dicks, anyway. Don't trust them. Wot's it worth? "

" What have you got? "

" Who's buying? " asked the little man.

" I don't know. Anyone else in the market? "

The smile came again, a little more reluctantly.

" You're tough," said the little man. " Five dahn, fifteen if the tip's okay."

Martin said, " All right," and sat down in his own chair; it had arms, but was not upholstered.

" What's your name? "

He opened his wallet and selected five pound notes. There were only six altogether, but he didn't show the man that.

" Rennie."

" Prove it."

Martin put the notes on the desk in front of him. The man who called himself Rennie put his hand to his own pocket, brought out a wallet which was unexpectedly new, and had probably been stolen recently, and from this took a dog-eared, dirty greenish card. He flipped this across the desk. Martin opened it, and read the name

79

and the address—William Rennie, 5 Moor Grove, Wapping; it was a National Registration Card.

Martin folded the notes inside the card and pushed them across the desk. They quickly disappeared into the wallet.

" Well, what is it? "

" I was doing a job night before larst," said Rennie, and the hoarse note seemed worse in his voice. " Putney. Near the river, I'd looked in to see some friends o' mine in a big 'ouse wiv grounds that stretch dahn to the river! " He grinned. " Comin' away, I see a couple of men standin' at the end of a jetty. You know, jetty."

" I know."

" They was dumpin' somefink," said Rennie. " In a sack. Made a big splash. They never see me, there was plenty of trees nearby, I stood in the shadders. One said to the ovver, ' okay,' 'e said, ' I'll git back to Buckley Street. I'll let you know about the rest to-morrow.' That's wot he said. Buckley Street, see? When I 'ad a dekko at the piper this morning, wot do I see? Plenty abaht Buckley Street, and that guy was going back there. 'Ow's that, guv'nor? "

Martin said, " What's worth twenty pounds? "

" Strike a light, in a n'urry, ain'tcha? " Rennie leaned forward and breathed heavily, and the laughter in his eyes seemed to flame. " I recognized the voice of the other guy, guv'nor."

" Sure? "

" Sure's I'm sittin' 'ere."

" Who is he, and where can I find him? "

" I'm takin' you on trust, mister, I dunno you won't welsh me. But I'll take a chance, I like yer face. 'E's *H*icky Sharp. Hicky's well known dahn our way, wouldn't s'prise me if the perlice don't know 'im, too." Rennie's grin was tight-lipped, but still showed that sense of humour that made him tolerable. " *H*icky's no good. Slit 'is own muvver's froat for 'arf a bar, 'e would, an' laugh doin' it. Bin on the level, 'e *says*, since 'e come aht larst time."

" Come out of where? "

" Cheese it, guv'nor. Jug. Inside."

" Sure he has a record? "

" Long as my arm," affirmed Rennie.

" All right," said Martin. " I'll check this, and if Hicky Sharp was at Putney on Wednesday night you'll get the extra fifteen. I'll have to be sure."

" I'll trust yer, fahsands wouldn't," said Rennie. " Just send me a postcard, and I'll come and collect the dough any time you like. Not 'ere, though, somewhere in the street. You say where."

" Right."

" Listen," said Rennie, leaning forward and breathing noisily into Martin's face, " you'll take this to the dicks, guv'nor, but keep my name aht of it. See? If you let me dahn——"

" I won't let you down."

" Just watch your step," said Rennie.

He stood up—and offered his hand; the nails were black, and the hand itself hadn't been washed for days. Martin shook it. Rennie grinned, and stood aside as Martin went to open the door for him. Barbara was alone in the outer office, and pretended not to notice Rennie. Rennie did not pretend not to notice her, but looked her up and down and grinned.

The door was locked.

" Let Mr. Rennie out, Miss Marrison, will you? "

" Yes, Mr. Fane." Barbara unlocked the door, Rennie touched his cap, winked at her, and went off. Barbara locked the door again and came hurrying to Martin, her excitement showing in her eyes. " Scoop, I heard some of it, was it genuine? "

" I think so—and this is where you're going to be the really important partner, you know the ropes! What's the rule if you get information which the police wouldn't get direct? Do you tell them right away? Or is it safe to hold it and try and get results yourself? "

Barbara said quietly, " There isn't any rule. You use

your own judgment. In this case I'd tell Kelby right away—it's dangerous, Scoop."

" It could be."

" It is—anything to do with murder is," insisted Barbara. " Robinson always passed on dangerous information, unless there was a special reason for holding it. Once he didn't, and—well, you know what happened. Legally—well, we haven't a special legal status in England, you don't have to be licensed to run a private inquiry agency. I've told you that. But if the police discovered that you'd been holding out on them they might turn nasty. They could probably close you up, and in any case they wouldn't be helpful. As it is they're well disposed, and they'd probably be tolerant and even helpful at times. If you gave them a genuine clue about the Clarke case you'd prove that you were going to play ball with them. Play ball, Scoop."

Barbara could not have been more earnest.

Martin considered.

" All right," he said at last. " But we'll check one or two things first. Do you know how to find out if there's an ex-convict named Hicky Sharp who lives at Wapping? He's supposed to have been inside several times, and to have been pretending to be on the level for the past few months or so."

Barbara hesitated.

" If there is such a man, my chap probably told the truth. If there isn't, it's cost me a fiver."

Barbara said, " I can find out, but the quickest way is to see Kelby. Darling, don't think I'm being too cautious. It's important to have the police friendly. There's no need to tell Kelby why you want to know, until you've found out about this man Sharp. If we were on the telephone I'd ring him up. You could slip out to a call-box and make sure he's in, and then——"

The telephone bell rang.

Martin started; Barbara glanced towards the instrument unbelievingly. It rang again—a long peal. Martin went towards it slowly. It had certainly been dead when they had taken it over. He lifted it.

" Hallo."

" Is that the office of Prince? "

" Speaking."

" This is the Telephone Exchange, sir, I'm testing your line. Can you hear me? "

" Perfectly," breathed Martin.

" Your number is Temple Bar 66331," said the operator. " Will you make a note of that? Temple Bar 66331."

Martin scribbled.

" Thank you very much," he said fervently.

" That's all right, sir. Goodbye."

The girl rang off, Martin stared at the scribbled number and then at Barbara—and as they were standing and looking at each other, the front-office bell rang. Barbara drew in a deep breath.

" That *can't* be another customer."

" Better see," said Martin.

He went towards the door, Barbara stood with a hand at her forehead. A man's shadow appeared beyond the frosted glass, and as Martin touched the key the bell rang again. He turned the key and opened the door, and Richard stood looking at him, head on one side, scowling.

" Doesn't this office ever open? "

" Come in, miracle worker," said Martin.

Richard grinned.

" Telephone people been through already? We had some luck—I happened to know the Johnny who handles this section, and there'd been a mistake, the line hadn't been disconnected at this end. So he waved a few wands, and promised we'd be on by midday. What's the number? "

Martin told him.

" I book the first call," said Richard, and made a bee-line for the telephone. " There are two extensions, but he's promised to put another line in for us this week with luck, next week for certain." He sat on the desk and

83

dialled. " This is really important business! Hallo— hallo, Kath! Guess who's speaking."

He listened; and looked fatuous.

" Right," he said after a pause. " How are you? Barbara says you had a good night. I'd have called before if I hadn't been sure of that."

He listened again, and chuckled.

" Yes, we're in business! Come and have a look at the office, if you can tear yourself away from Ching."

He held on for a moment longer, added:

" Fine, I'll be seeing you," and rang off. " If a young lady comes asking for me, it'll be Miss Kathleen Wilder, and I'll see her right away. Well, well, well! " He looked round the office, went across to the doorways, peeped inside each room, clapped his hands together, came straight to Barbara and took her in his arms, and began to hum a quick-step and dance to the tune. " Aren't we all wonderful, Bar? You and even Martin. Office—staff—had any customers yet? "

Martin kept a straight face.

" Yes, a man looking for a gold watch."

" Found it for him yet? "

" No," said Barbara. " He lost it on a bus near Fulham Palace Road last night—got on near the Rose and Crown and off at Putney Bridge, on the Fulham side, and swears he had it before he left the pub and after he reached the bus. He left the Rose and Crown just after closing time, so you should be able to find the bus and have a word with the conductor."

" Twenty to one in cigarettes that you don't find the watch," said Martin.

" Won't I! Lost Property Office——"

" It happened last Friday, and every normal channel, as they say, has been explored."

" Just leave it to me," said Richard easily. " Anything else? "

" A woman offered us a divorce case, but I turned it down," said Barbara.

84

Martin murmured, " A man offered to lead me to Mrs. Clarke's murderer, and I——"

" What? "   Richard looked appalled.   " Did you turn that——"

" Not quite, and it'll cost the firm twenty pounds if it comes off," said Martin.   " That reminds me, I must telephone Scotland Yard.   Unless you've any more urgent calls to make, Skip."

" You carry on," said Richard heavily, and appealed to Barbara: " Is he fooling? "

" Oh, no."

Martin lifted the telephone, hesitated, and then felt an absurd excitement as he began to dial Whitehall 1212.

11

RICHARD sat on the corner of Martin's desk, swinging his legs, and Barbara sat at her typewriter, looking at Martin with a rapt expression which brought a smile to Richard's eyes. Scotland Yard lost no time in answering; soon Kelby was on the line. Martin fancied that the Superintendent's hearty greeting meant that his tongue was still in his cheek; he was doubtless amused by this venture.

" Hallo, Mr. Fane, want our help already? "

" I'd like your advice," said Martin.

" Always glad to dispense advice," Kelby said. " By the way, I went round to see Wimple after I left you this morning, and he asked me to say he won't forget how much he owes you."

" Oh, that's all right."

" Now what's the trouble? "

" Do you happen to know of a man named Hicky Sharp? He lives in the East End somewhere, and I'm told he has a record."

Kelby chuckled.

" Don't get yourself mixed up with men like Hicky Sharp, Mr. Fane. Hicky's a nasty piece of work—the type who'd gladly cut his own mother's throat for a bottle of Scotch. How did you come to hear of him? "

" Well—it's a little difficult to talk over the telephone. Can you spare me half an hour? I think you'll find it worth your while."

" Er—when? "

Kelby wasn't enthusiastic.

" Right away."

" I'm afraid I can't," said Kelby. " I've several appointments and a lot of desk work to clear up. I could

86

manage it to-morrow morning, unless something crops up, or——"

" This might give us a line on the Clarke business," Martin said, almost casually.

" *What* did you say? "

" The Clarke business."

There was a pause; and when he spoke again Kelby's voice held a very different note.

" You're sure about this, I suppose? "

" I think so."

" All right, come along at once. I'll tell them in the hall to bring you right up. Come to the new building— you know it, don't you? "

" Oh, yes. Thanks."

Martin put the receiver down, Barbara jumped up and came across to him, while Richard, who was looking very thoughtful, glanced from one to the other and didn't speak.

" Just right," Barbara said. " You played him beautifully. Richard, you'll probably want to kick me, but if I were you I'd leave Scoop to deal with Scotland Yard. He has just the right manner with them, where you might get their backs up."

" Yes, ma'am. But what is all this about a Hicky Sharp and the Clarke case? I thought you were fooling when you first said you'd a line. What's happened? "

Barbara said, " You'd better go off, Scoop, don't keep Kelby waiting. I'll tell Richard."

" Now wait a minute." Richard stood up, and put a brotherly hand on Barbara's shoulder. " You could be making a mistake about the approach to the Yard. We don't need to eat out of their hands. It won't do Kelby any harm to wait for ten minutes, he won't know how long it took to get across to the Yard, anyhow. Tell me in your own fair words, Scoop."

Martin shrugged.

" There isn't much to tell." He told it all in a very few minutes. " Now I'll get along, I'm on Barbara's side about dealing with the Yard."

"You'll both learn," said Richard, and shrugged. "All right, I'll be office boy! We have to get some letter-heading printed, we ought to have some cards, and believe it or not, someone forgot the ink, pens, and blotting-paper this morning, as well as the stationery oddments—rubber bands and things. Also, we ought to have a boy or a girl, someone young, to answer the telephone and all that kind of thing, oughtn't we? Shall I see what I can do?"

"I shouldn't add to the staff yet," advised Barbara.

"We'll go into conference about that later," said Richard, and followed Martin to the door. "It's your turn for the car, old chap, isn't it?"

"Thanks," said Martin dryly.

"Oh, don't mention it." They went downstairs together, and Richard began to chuckle. "You know, Scoop, few people would believe that you really got behind this thing and drove it so far. You make the world think that it takes a month for you to make up your mind on anything. In fact, you make me look like a snail when you're really on the move. How do you feel about things?"

"It could be big. We've had a fine start."

"Wonderful! Even squealers walk into the office and ladle out information." They stepped into the Strand, where a few flakes of snow were falling, carried about by the blustery wind. Everyone looked cold, noses were red, the taxi-drivers were bundled up in an incredible thickness of coats. "Going to chance driving?" asked Richard. "The road's up in Trafalgar Square. Probably the best way would be for you to nip down to the Square and get the tube. It takes you practically on the Yard's doorstep."

The Buick was parked round the corner, its cream paint in need of a wash. Martin looked at it and then at Richard, and slowly shook his head.

"It's my turn for the car. Remember?"

Richard grinned.

"I surrender."

" And remember," said Martin firmly, " that I like green blotting-paper."

Richard waved and walked briskly off, towards Fleet Street and the City. Martin took the wheel, but glanced back at his brother. He had an uneasy feeling that Richard had been carried away by some bright notion; it was difficult to guess what it was. Probably he had a girl in mind for the office job; but for his obvious seriousness about Kathleen Wilder, Martin would have felt sure that was the explanation. Certainly he was not in such a hurry simply to go and buy a few oddments of stationery.

Martin shrugged his shoulders and drove off.

He was lucky with the traffic, and turned off the Embankment into the courtyard of the new building of Scotland Yard, in a flurry of snow which swept towards him from the river. The roads and pavements were already filmed with white. He pulled up alongside several other cars, a constable on duty saluted, and at the top of the stairs a bare-headed sergeant greeted him affably.

" Good morning, sir."

" Superintendent Kelby said that he would see me."

" Mr. Fane? "

" Yes."

" Just fill in this form, sir, will you? " The sergeant turned to a small table, handed Martin a buff form and a pencil, and, as he filled in brief details of his reason for calling, beckoned a constable. " The constable will take you up, sir."

" Thanks."

Martin followed the constable along the wide passages. He felt—as he had when he had first come here some six months ago—an almost boyish thrill at the thought that he was walking through the passages of the Criminal Investigation Department, now housed in the new building. Heavily built men in plain clothes passed him, one or two stared as if in recognition. They reached a lift, were taken to the second floor; a nearby door was ajar, and Kelby's voice sounded:

". . . and if the Liverpool boys can't do anything, try Glasgow. Okay, Dickie."

A big man came out of the office as the constable led the way to it.

" Mr. Fane, sir."

" Oh, yes. Come in, Mr. Fane."

Kelby was sitting at a large desk at one end of a long room; another desk, opposite his, was empty. In spite of the cold and the steam heat from radiators, two of the windows were open. The snow was still falling fast, and much more was settling than when Martin had come in. Kelby rose a few inches from his chair, and waved to one in front of the desk. The constable closed the door.

The desk was only just large enough to hold the papers, books, telephones, and oddments which were on it. It was crowded but not untidy. Kelby sat with his back to the wall, and his head hid part of a long picture of rows and rows of policemen in uniform.

Kelby offered cigarettes from a battered packet.

" Thanks."

Martin lit up.

" Shall we get one thing straight, Mr. Fane? " Kelby was serious, in spite of a smile. " You've started a new kind of business for yourself, and we've nothing against that. There's a lot that private agencies can do, but there are a lot of things that they can't and shouldn't—work best left to us. We're experts. We're trained, too—you'd be surprised how much training a man has to go through before he can become a detective officer. One or two agencies have a sad habit of biting off more than they can chew, and one of them was the Robinson Agency. Remember? Miss Marrison worked a great deal with Robinson, and he was murdered because he thought he could be clever and tackle a job that ought to have been handed over to us."

Martin nodded.

"We like to be on good terms with anyone who's running an agency, and we can help each other—*if* we both go the right way about it. I know we owe you a lot because of what happened last night, don't misunderstand me. I just want you to know what we think."

Martin's eyes crinkled at the corners.

"I'm beginning to see," he said lightly. "What you really mean is, don't tell you half a story, tell you everything."

Kelby rubbed his hands together.

"It's a pleasure to deal with someone who's so quick on the uptake, Mr. Fane. Just one other thing. I'm not very worried about you or Miss Marrison—she learned her lesson, and you're a thoughtful kind of chap. I'm a bit worried about your brother. He probably won't listen to reason and may get some crack-brained notion that he can do a job better than we can. Try to make sure he isn't too impulsive, will you? I remember him from the other affair—and I also remember that both of you finished that off yourselves and told us about it afterwards. There was a pretty good excuse, but——"

He broke off.

"We'll always be sure there's a good excuse," said Martin. "Are you interested in the Clarke case?"

Kelby grinned.

"All right, I asked for that." He was casual again; and was saying, as clearly as he could, that he didn't think that the information would be worth a great deal, and that in any case he was going to make sure in advance that Martin did not have any reason to think that it was of major importance. "Well, what's it all about?"

Martin stubbed out his cigarette, and said deliberately:

"My information is that Mrs. Clarke's body was dumped into the river off a private jetty at Putney on Wednesday night. There were two men. One of the men was Hicky Sharp."

As the words came out Kelby's expression altered; the change was almost ludicrous. His deliberate attempt to treat the matter in advance as if it were only incidental was stillborn. He gulped twice, and hadn't any immediate comment to make when Martin had finished. Actually he leaned forwards, glanced away from Martin, and then looked back, a sideways glance. His fleshy face and the rather small eyes looked positively ugly.

" I see," he said at last. " Were you there ? "

" No. I had the information from a man who knows Hicky Sharp, and was doing a job near the river at the time."

" Who's the man ? "

" He gave me his name in confidence, and I can't betray a client's confidence."

Kelby began to beat a tattoo on the desk, and now looked straight into Martin's eyes. Martin couldn't be sure how he felt about that refusal to pass on information ; then he leaned forward, lifted a telephone, and said, " Get me Putney." He held the receiver to his ear, and looked at Martin with his small eyes still shadowed, as if with doubt and surprise. It was a long time before he spoke again, and the atmosphere in the office seemed to get heavy and tense. Then :

" Hello—oh, hallo, Mark. This is Bob Kelby. . . . Have much trouble your way the night before last ? Near the river. . . . Oh, did you ? Any of the places with private jetties ? . . . I see . . . Any idea who did the job ? . . . Sure it was an old hand ? . . . Well, listen. Get a squad down to the river, cordon off the jetty, look out for all the usual stuff. Will you hurry ? I think Mrs. Clarke was dumped off from one of those jetties. I'll come down myself as soon as I can, and if I'm delayed I'll send Oakes. . . . Yes, I think so. Right-ho, old man."

He rang off.

" How did you get this information, Mr. Fane ? "

" A man called at the office."

" What did it cost you ? "

" Twenty pounds."

"When did you get it?"

"About ten minutes before I telephoned you."

"I see. Thanks. There was a burglary at one of the houses on the river-side at Putney the night before last, it looks as if you might have got something. If your informant had nothing to do with the murder, all right. If he had——"

"I'd name him."

"I think we understand each other," said Kelby, and stood up.

Martin didn't move.

"Don't tell me you have something else," said Kelby.

"Not yet." Martin's smile was almost naïve. "I hope to have a little more soon, Superintendent. Haven't I earned a little information? Why were you searching Clarke's flat so thoroughly last night?"

Kelby frowned and sat down again.

"You keep your eyes open, don't you?"

"You were going through drawers and cupboards, turning everything out," said Martin. "Just routine?"

"No," said Kelby slowly. "No, it wasn't just routine last night. The Press will probably get hold of this soon, but I'll give it you now in confidence. We were looking for slush."

He paused, as if hoping that he would be asked to translate.

"Counterfeit," murmured Martin.

"Forged notes. We've been after Mr. Clarke for that for some weeks. There's a lot of slush on the market, especially on the Continent and in the United States. Much more than usual, and we're sure that it's being printed in London. Clarke was a paper-manufacturer in a small way, and we've discovered that he's been making paper which is almost indistinguishable from the paper on which one-pound and ten-shilling notes are printed. It has a cotton thread, too. He hasn't been on the job for the past few days. But keep that to yourself, Mr. Fane."

" Did you find any at Buckley Street? "

Kelby grinned as he shook his head.

" But we'll find it, don't worry about that. Turn over all the money in your wallet and make sure it's good, Mr. Fane! The drawing of this slush is first-rate, and the blocks can't be faulted. Bit of an artist yourself, by the way, aren't you? "

MARTIN hurried up the stone steps leading to the office at Quill House. Barbara was sitting at one of the desks, talking to a young woman in a scarlet coat and with a feather so tall that it seemed to reach half-way to the ceiling. Barbara glanced up at him.

" I won't be long."

" That's all right."

Martin went into his own office, sat back, and stared at the blank wall of the building opposite. Kelby had only been joking, of course, but had given him a nasty turn. Probably Kelby was, at heart, opposed to amateurs meddling; there were exceptional circumstances here which forced him to be reasonable, but he couldn't keep his dislike of amateurs out completely.

He certainly couldn't have been serious. Could he?

Footsteps sounded on the bare boards of the office, and the outer door opened and closed. Barbara came in.

" We'll have to get something for the floor, Scoop, it sounds dreadful. Most of the boards creak, anyhow. How did you get on? "

" It's a counterfeit—I mean forgery—business. Clarke made the paper, apparently. Kelby made a nasty crack about my drawing, and said that the artistry on these notes is perfect and the blocks can't be faulted. That doesn't matter much, but it shook me."

" I see," said Barbara slowly. " No, I suppose it doesn't matter much. It might give Kelby an excuse for asking you not to do anything more in the case. I don't know. Kelby's the one I like least over there. He's all right, fair as they come, but he doesn't like private agencies.

We'll just have to be careful with him. He's good, there's no doubt about that."

" And quick." Martin told her what had happened. " And shrewd," he added. " He knows that if he's going to have any trouble, it will be with Richard."

Barbara's eyes danced.

" I almost hope he has a little! I wonder how long Richard will be? "

" He's probably explaining to someone why he can't give her a job in the office to-day," said Martin.

" Unless he's gone to try to get that gold watch! "

Martin's chuckle came explosively.

" Great Scott, yes! I could see he was turning something over in his mind, preparing some kind of bombshell. It wouldn't surprise me if he turns up with the watch. What did the feather want? "

" Autographs! "

The outer office door opened as they laughed, and the telephone bell rang at the same time. Barbara went out, Martin picked up the telephone, heard the noise of pennies dropping into the call box, and then his father's voice.

" Is Mr. Fane there? "

" Hallo, Dad! "

" Hallo, Scoop. How are things going? "

" Fine! "

" Good. Don't get too excited at the start, though. Your mother's on her way now, she's just left me in Arundel Street. I had to come along and see Matthew for half an hour, but she couldn't rest until she'd seen you and Richard. I'll be along by half-past twelve. Are you free for lunch? "

" I think so."

" Well, try and make it—you or Richard," said Fane. " Mother's out for Richard's blood, by the way. Tell him to be sensible, won't you? "

Martin now knew why his father had called.

" Yes. Everyone is gunning for Richard this morning.

He'll probably buy a bullet-proof waistcoat. You'll be here at half-past twelve, then."

" Yes."

Fane rang off, and Martin put down the receiver as Barbara came in from the outer office. Barbara was looking puzzled. Martin paused, and enjoyed looking at her, especially the way she brushed a few strands of hair back from her forehead, in a preoccupied fashion which was characteristic of her.

" Trouble? " he asked.

" Not really. A young floozie who calls herself Fifi——"

" Fifi! "

" That's right, the finder of lost dogs," said Barbara, with a smile which was still a little puzzled. " She said that Kathleen Wilder will be here by twelve o'clock, and that she *must* see Richard. If Fifi is right, Kathleen's badly worried about something. I can't imagine what."

Martin rubbed his chin slowly, and didn't say whether he could imagine anything that might still worry Kathleen.

" I wonder where Richard is," Barbara said again, and laughed. " I——"

" Do you mean to say he's not *here*? " The voice came from the outer door, and Barbara turned round quickly and Martin jumped up from his desk. Evelyn Fane came walking across the office, and stood in the doorway. She wore a wine-red suit with a wide-brimmed white hat, white gloves trimmed with red, red shoes and carried a fur coat. She was perfectly made up, and looked years less than her age.

" I want to see *Master* Richard."

She smiled at them both.

Martin rounded the desk.

" He'll soon be back, he's gone out to buy some blotting-paper. Hallo, Mother! You look as if Dad let you loose in Bond Street. Or was it Harrods? "

" How *do* you manage to dress so perfectly? " Barbara said. " You're a walking Dior model."

Evelyn's eyes twinkled; and soon became frosty.

" If you think you're going to smooth me down with a few careless compliments, you're both wrong. I think this business is ridiculous, and I always shall. Hallo, Barbara." She put her face forward, and they touched cheeks; quickly but warmly, there was genuine affection between them.

Martin kissed his mother lightly.

" We'll be all right," he said. " We've had half a dozen customers already this morning."

" That's just a false start," said Evelyn sceptically. " Well, it's done now, and I suppose you'll have to wait until you've lost all your money before you'll admit that I was right. You *must* have some carpet on the floor or you'll never get anyone to come twice."

" Yes——" began Barbara.

" We can't afford it," said Martin quickly but firmly. " In a couple of months' time we may be able to manage it. It's what we offer from here "—he tapped his forehead—" that really matters, not the comfort we give to tired feet. But come and sit down, you hate standing."

Evelyn sat down in the client's chair.

" Did your father ring up? "

" Yes."

" I thought he would, the moment my back was turned," said Evelyn. " I'll bet he wanted to have a word with Richard and warn him about my coming." Her eyes sparkled, but there was a touch of real anxiety in them. " Martin's no judge, but you ought to know, Barbara. What's this girl like? "

" Well—— "

" So you don't like her," Evelyn flashed.

Martin chuckled.

" No wonder Richard's impulsive! "

" Be quiet, Martin, I was asking Barbara. You *don't* like her, do you? "

" I was going to say that although I don't know her well, I like what I've seen of her very much indeed. I

98

think you will, too. Martin has the same impression. Of course, it's all in the air, we're not at all certain that anything will come of it. You know Richard!"

" That's my chief worry," said Evelyn fervently.

" You'll soon know what she's like," Martin said. " She's coming here at twelve o'clock—that's in five minutes or so—to see Richard."

" Oh, *is* she?" Evelyn stood up and went to the door. She glanced round the outer office, and said firmly, " When she comes, *I'll* see her by myself. You two can stay in here, and neither of you can warn her who I am. I shall know the moment I set eyes on her whether I like her or not."

" I'm sure you will," Barbara said.

" What time did you say? Twelve?"

" Yes."

" Don't forget, you're both to stay in here," ordered Evelyn. " Afterwards I'll go into another room, that one across there, and if I *don't* like her, woe betide you." She came back to the desk, kicked against a board which stood up slightly above the others, and stumbled. Barbara put out a hand to steady her. " Are you *insured?*" Evelyn asked coldly.

" We shall be, but——"

" I can't understand you, Martin," said Evelyn. " I thought you were level-headed and sensible, if no one else was. You're going to say that there hasn't been time to look after insurance, but surely it's the first thing you ought to do. You can always get a cover, or something, can't you?"

" The chief trouble with you," said Martin cheerfully, " is that you're nearly always right. I'll have a word with someone right away—who are the best people, Bar? Do you know?"

" Coverall Insurance," said Barbara promptly. " Ask for Mr. White."

" It takes you women!" Martin slipped his arm round his mother's shoulder, and hugged her. " We'll

99

get through this very nicely, thanks to Prince. Have you seen the newspapers? "

" I'd have had a job not to. Your father buys every newspaper that's printed, and would get any left over from yesterday if he could, then just skims through the headlines and pretends that he's read them."

" They did us proud, didn't they? "

Evelyn laughed, and looked lovely.

" Yes, very. Scoop, be careful. You might have fallen and broken your neck last night, from what I can see from the reports. At least you've made Scotland Yard friendly, that's something. When do you expect Richard back? "

" Any minute."

" I hope that girl comes before he does. What did you say her name is? "

" Kathleen Wilder."

" You can't tell from names," mused Evelyn. " I suppose your father will ask her to have lunch with us, if he arrives before she goes. He's too soft. He——"

Evelyn broke off as the outer door opened. She got up quickly, and was at the nearer door a long time before Martin. Barbara stood aside to let her pass. She pushed the door to behind her, but didn't close it, made a face which was half-frown, half-smile, and stepped into the outer office.

A younger woman was coming in.

" Is Richard in? " the caller asked quickly. " I must see him at once, it's terribly urgent."

Evelyn Fane looked at her without speaking, then turned and darted a searing glance towards the door. Both Barbara and Martin saw that; and Barbara gulped. Never had scorn and righteous indignation shown more clearly on a human face than on Evelyn's. For she took it for granted that this was Kathleen Wilder.

In fact it was Rosa Harding.

.   .   .   .   .

Rosa was not looking at her best. Her nose was red

from the cold, she wore an old fur coat, worn badly at the sleeves, and a scarf round her head. She could not prevent herself from looking striking—or her manner from being imperious to a point of arrogance.

"Is he in? I must see him."

"*I* have nothing to do with this establishment," said Evelyn coldly. "You had better wait until one of the— of the *clerks* comes out."

She turned on her heel, and swept into the smaller office. Martin and Barbara backed away as Evelyn slammed the door and then leaned her back against it. Rosa had found a buzzer on the counter and was pressing it furiously; the ringing sound wasn't loud, certainly not loud enough to drown Evelyn's whisper.

"What on earth is the matter with you both? *Nice?* That woman's a termagant, a shrew, a devil, I wouldn't trust her an inch. Not for a minute. If Richard's serious about her he must have taken leave of his senses, and if you two have encouraged him——"

She broke off, for floor-boards creaked; the buzzer had stopped buzzing. Martin stretched out a hand and drew his mother from the door as Rosa thrust it open violently, strode in, and said:

"Why don't you answer the bell? Where's Richard? I must see him. Kathleen has been kidnapped."

13

No one spoke. Rosa glared round from one to the other, and the look she gave Evelyn was obviously of acute dislike; that was mutual. She flung back her scarf, so that it dropped to her shoulder, and her chin was thrust forward. But for her red nose she would have been strikingly attractive ; and she had a splendid figure.

" Are you dumb? Where is Richard ? "

" What on earth are you talking about? " asked Barbara. " Who said that Kathleen had been kidnapped ? "

" *I* say so."

" What on earth is happening? " demanded Evelyn, moving towards the desk as if she were in need of support. " Who is this woman ? "

" A friend of Kathleen's," Martin said quickly. " Sit down, mother, we'll look after this. Miss Harding, we had a message about a quarter of an hour ago saying that Kathleen would be here at twelve o'clock. How can she——"

" *I* sent the message through Fifi. I wasn't sure that Richard would see me, he's never liked me, so I made the appointment in Kath's name. *I'm* genuinely fond of Kathleen. I was out for an hour, giving Ching a walk— I daren't let him out of the flat without a lead after what happened last night. When I got back Kath had gone. A few minutes afterwards a man telephoned and said that if I wanted to see her again I must go and see *him*. I went to see him at Piccadilly Circus, but told Fifi—she was with me—to come and see you. I had to make sure *one* of you was in. Then I rushed here by ta⁀i. I've left poor Ching with friends, and——"

" What did the man say? " demanded Martin.

" That Kathleen would be all right if I kept away from the police and if you took your nose out of other people's affairs. *And* he's right. Of all the silly ideas, starting a private inquiry agency! Kathleen will have nothing to do with anyone who has anything to do with this, if I have *my* way."

Evelyn, sitting down, was breathing through her nostrils, and staring with increasing hostility towards Rosa.

Martin said, " Wait a minute. What was the man like? "

" He was just a man. Nothing much. I couldn't see much of him, anyhow, he was so bundled up in clothes."

" Is that all he said? "

" Yes."

Even the single word was aggressive.

" Well, well," said Martin. " Barbara, I'll be back as soon as I can. I may have to miss lunch, Mum, sorry. I'll see you some time."

He went out of the office like a flash, snatching his coat from a peg in the wall as he went, and the door slammed behind him. Consequently he did not hear Evelyn say stonily:

" I don't know who you are, but if my sons wish to open a legitimate business I don't see what affair it is of yours."

" Don't you? " Rosa's voice was icy. " Kathleen is a friend of mine, and apparently your son——"

Barbara raised her voice. " Have you told the police?"

" I have not."

" *Why* not? " demanded Evelyn in a dangerously soft voice. " Isn't kidnapping a matter for the police? "

" This man said——"

" You must have taken leave of your senses," said Evelyn. " Barbara, please inform the police at once."

She looked at the telephone.

" You will not." Rosa strode across the room and

stood so that anyone who wanted to use the telephone would have to push her aside. " I don't want any harm to come to Kathleen, and the man was most emphatic— I was not to tell the police, but I was to tell the Fane brothers to keep their noses out of this. I'd already warned Kathleen to be careful of Richard, and now that he's cashing in with all this cheap publicity——"

" Cheap! " breathed Evelyn.

Barbara said quietly, " Mother, leave this to me, please."

Evelyn shrugged, and went regally out of the office. Barbara leaned forward, and stared up in Rosa Harding's eyes. Rosa seemed suddenly to grow weak, went to a chair, and dropped into it; she was trembling. There was no possible doubt that she was frightened.

If she could be believed, she knew nothing more than she had already said.

.　　.　　.　　.　　.

Martin reached the street, where he waved to two taxis which passed, ignoring him. The Buick was some distance off, and he plunged across the slippery road. An inch of snow lay on it now, but was beginning to melt, and the snow had stopped falling. A bus braked sharply to avoid him. He reached the opposite pavement and ran towards Charing Cross Station, then turned down towards the Adelphi. Buckley Street was only ten minutes' walk from the office, but it seemed to take him an age to get there.

He turned into the house, and hurried up the stairs; and told himself that he had probably made a mistake. He was behaving like Richard, acting on an impulse which had no real justification. Yet one thing had seemed certain; someone had been determined to get both Kathleen and Rosa out of their flat and had succeeded. An idea which had filtered into his mind when he had been sitting opposite Kelby had become stronger after he had heard Rosa's story.

No one was on the top landing. Someone had added a

little more to the repairs, and the temporary banisters now looked much stronger. He had expected to find a policeman on duty here; presumably he was inside the Clarkes' flat, the front door of which was ajar. Martin walked quickly up to No. 6.

The lock on the door was not a Yale; it could be opened with a skeleton key as easily as Clarke's front door. Martin stepped close to the door, listened, and fancied that he heard movements. He bent down and put his ear to the keyhole. There was no doubt about the movements of two or three people inside. Everything that Kelby had said came back with considerable force; and also everything Barbara had advised. But his fingers itched to use the skeleton key.

He took out the knife.

The rest of the building was so quiet that the sounds from the flat seemed loud.

He had only to go into No. 5 and tell the policeman that although the tenants of the flat were supposed to be out, someone was inside, and the man would act immediately. There could be no doubt about the wise thing to do.

He opened the knife and started to use the skeleton key. Inwardly he felt calmer than he had expected. The lock turned, making surprisingly little noise. There was a slight click as it went back, and he paused, listening. He heard a sound that might have been a drawer opening.

He pushed the door open a few inches and looked inside.

Two men were kneeling with their backs towards him. The fitted carpet had been pulled up at the far end of the room and along part of each side, and rolled back. The men, wearing blue dungarees, were unscrewing floorboards, and three floorboards were already up. The men each had a big canvas tool-bag; and by the side of one of these was a pile of treasury notes. There were four or five bundles of notes, two so high that they toppled to one side.

Martin drew back and pulled the door to, but didn't close it, for fear of making a noise. He stood quite still on the landing. Richard would probably say he'd had a hunch; it didn't matter what anyone called it, but he had struck lucky again. Kelby had searched Clarke's flat for the forged notes, and they had been hidden here. He had seen several hundred, perhaps a thousand; it was anyone's guess how many more were under the boards.

This implicated Rosa and Kathleen; at least, it could implicate them. He had no personal interest in either, but Richard had plenty. If Richard felt half as strongly as he did about Barbara, Richard would feel bad over this. And Rosa had tried to stop him and Richard from taking any further interest in the case.

The sounds came more clearly now; he judged that another floorboard had come up, and guessed that there would be several others to come. He touched the handle of the door again, then drew back. Closing the door might attract their attention more quickly than if he left it just open; there wasn't likely to be much wind up here to close it noisily in a draught. Martin knew exactly what he had to do now, although Richard wouldn't like it. He gently pushed open the door of the Clarkes' flat.

A constable sprang up from a chair and opened his mouth. Martin put his finger to his lips.

" Two men in flat No. 6," he said softly. " Tearing up floorboards. Did you see them go in? "

" You mean the gas fitters——"

" They aren't working on gas now. Did you know both the tenants of the flat are out? "

" No, I didn't—look here, who do you think——"

" Fane is the name. If the men come out, hold them. If you don't, Superintendent Kelby will probably have the pants off you. I'm going to telephone him."

. . . . .

Kelby wasn't there; a Chief Inspector Oakes spoke to

Martin, listened, had little to say, said that he would check the report. Martin, speaking from a telephone kiosk at the end of Buckley Street, put down the receiver moodily, and hoped he had done the right thing. He could picture Kathleen Wilder, and the way Richard had looked at her. If Kathleen were mixed up with this business Richard wouldn't have a good time.

He lit a cigarette. Another squall of snow came fiercely, and he turned his back against the driving wind. It soon steadied, but another powdering of snow covered the streets. After three minutes he heard the engine of a car, looked round, and saw a police patrol car swing round the corner. It stopped by the policeman, but the men didn't get out until a second car came from another direction and pulled up. Then two men climbed out of each and went into the house.

Martin didn't wait to see anything more.

. . . . .

"Martin! Hey, Martin!"

Martin recognized his father's voice when about to turn into the entrance to the office building. He turned round eagerly. Jonathan Fane was leaning out of the window of a taxi which was drawing up. He climbed out, shook hands with Martin and paid the cabby, and they walked together towards the door. Fane walked carefully and with a slight limp. He looked fresh, and his eyes were bright and eager; the quality of youthfulness was in both him and his wife.

"Well, how did it go?"

"Not as you'd expect," said Martin slowly. "Look here, let's have a chat before we go upstairs. There are some chairs along the passage here."

He had noticed the chairs earlier, at the end of a passage which led off the front hall. Fane, looking thoughtfully into his son's face, didn't argue. They sat down, and Martin talked in a low-pitched voice; he left nothing out. Fane raised one eyebrow two or three times, but didn't once interrupt.

107

Martin took out his cigarette-case and proffered it.

" I'm not sure whether I did the right thing. It's an astonishing business. I can't believe Kathleen's mixed up in it, but—well, I'd put two and two together. I knew that Kelby was surprised that no forged notes were found at Clarke's flat. Then Rosa made it obvious that someone wanted both her and Kathleen out of the flat, and—well, I wondered why."

Fane chuckled comfortably, and Martin looked less worried.

" You think it was right? "

" My dear Scoop, only a fool—or Richard!—would have done anything different from that. If Kathleen's involved, this is the right time to find out. It would be a pity, I suppose—your mother probably wouldn't think so!—but he'd get over it. I wasn't laughing at that, though, I was marvelling at the way your mind works. I fancy you've found the right line of country. The Prince in real life—it must be hereditary! "

Martin grinned.

" Let's go up and ask Mother! "

" She'll agree," said Fane. " There's one thing that you didn't make clear," he added, as they went towards the staircase. " Did you tell the Yard about the kidnapping story? "

" Oh, yes. No sense in holding part of it back."

" You couldn't be more right. Half-truths won't get you anywhere. If you're going to withhold anything, withhold everything. There might come a time when you'll want to." They reached the second floor, and Fane was breathing rather heavily. " I was never any good at stairs. Hal-lo! " He stood opposite the front door, smiling at the single word PRINCE which was painted on it. " Almost like home." He squeezed Martin's arm. "I can't tell you how much I want this to be a success."

" Thanks."

" And when your mother's used to the idea, she'll feel the same."

108

Fane went across to the door, opened it, and heard Barbara speaking. He knew at once that there was trouble; he knew every intonation in Barbara's voice, could judge her mood from it unerringly. She was alarmed, almost desperate.

"No, he's not here. I'll tell him the moment he comes, but can't you give me an address? If——"

"For me?" Martin called swiftly from the door.

Barbara swung round from the telephone in the outer office as the men entered. Evelyn came hurrying from the desk, anxiety on her face and in her fine eyes.

"Hold on! He's here!" Barbara cried, and held out the telephone, while Evelyn said fiercely:

"It's some crook. He says that Richard's in trouble, but he won't speak to anyone but you. Hurry, Scoop."

Fane said, "*What?*"

"Be quiet!"

Martin took the telephone, forced himself to speak calmly, and sat on the corner of the desk, looking away from the senior Fanes.

"Is that you, Rennie?"

"Sure. Listen, guv'nor. That brother of yourn's going to get 'urt if you don't look snappy. 'E's at 5 Ribley Court, Wapping. You'd better get a move on."

14

RICHARD hurried round to a garage where he was known, and hired a rakish-looking Alvis with green bodywork. He drove back to the Strand, threading his way between the traffic; his driving was brilliant, and he throve on London conditions. As he reached Aldwych and the one-way turning, he mused aloud:

" My need was greater than yours this time, Scoop! "

He stayed with the main stream of cars and buses until he reached Ludgate Circus, then turned off towards Blackfriars Bridge, found the traffic less congested, and drove along towards the city, keeping as near to the river as he could. He reached the fringe of the East End, at Aldgate, and pulled into a side street near a public-house which was not yet open for business. He knocked at the side door. A pert-looking girl opened it, and her eyes lit up.

" Hallo, Mr. Fane! "

" Hallo, Lucy. Is Pop in? "

" Sure. Thirsty all of a sudden? "

" Now would I break the law? " asked Richard.

" And then some! "

Lucy laughed, as she led the way through a narrow passage, reeking with the smell of beer, to a small room at the back of the public rooms of the pub. Crates and barrels, all of them full, lined the walls; there was only just room for them to pass. The door of the room was open, and a man with a completely bald head sat at a table with papers spread out about him. He had a pencil in his hand and thick horn-rimmed glasses on his round face, and he was gnawing at the pencil.

" Gentleman to see you, Pop," said Lucy.

"Wot? Eh? Who?" The bald-headed man looked up worriedly. "Oh, Mr. Fane. Glad to see you." He put out his hand, but his smile was preoccupied. "Aren't any good at figuring, are you, Mr. Fane?"

"I'm useless," confessed Richard.

"So'm I. Once a month I have to do these accounts, otherwise I get into a hell of a mess in April with income tax. There ought to be a *law* against income tax!" His smile became more free, he tucked the pencil behind his ear and pushed the papers away; half a dozen fluttered to the floor. "That's enough of them for to-day."

"Now look what you've done. Don't I have to do enough bending?" Lucy demanded, and started to pick up the papers.

"None of your cheek, my girl. Well, Mr. Fane, what's brought you? Don't often see you in the daytime."

Richard smiled broadly.

"I'm reforming, Pop. I don't think I'll be writing any more stories about the East End for a while. I've started up a new business. Catching crooks and finding things."

Lucy straightened up, bumped her head on the corner of the table, winced but didn't cry out. She stood with papers in her hand, staring at Richard, lips parted, consternation in her eyes. Pop's eyes, looking small behind thick lenses, held the same expression. He was a pale and podgy man, and he pushed his chair back slowly from the table; it eased his stomach where it had pressed against the side.

"Come again," he said.

"Only my joke! But I'm interested in a man you might have heard of—you're the only one I know who knows practically everyone east of Aldgate Pump. I just want to check up on the fellow. His name's Sharp—Hicky Sharp."

Lucy sat down abruptly.

"Now listen to me, Mr. Fane," said Pop with careful emphasis, "don't you have anything to do with Hicky

Sharp. Of course I know him. He's bad. They don't come any worse. I don't know what your interest is, but keep away from him. I can't prevent him from coming in here, and he looks in sometimes, but I don't mind telling you I'm glad when he's gone. They just don't come any worse, Mr. Fane."

Richard looked astounded.

" As bad as that? "

" *Worse* than that."

" Does he live in London? "

" Why do you want to know? "

Richard wished he had not announced his impending resignation from *Charade*, but looked bland as he sat on the edge of the table, his leg swinging.

He laughed lightly.

" No need to look at me like that, Pop. I'm not going to try to make him mend his ways. As a matter of fact I've heard rumours about him, and I'd like to get a personal interview. It would be worth twenty pounds to him. Think you could arrange a meeting? "

" Not me," said Pop. " Twenty quid—well, I don't know how Hicky's fixed. I've known the time when he'd do a lot for twenty smackers, other times he would call it pin-money and give it away. He *might* see you. If you must try, see his daughter—she knows him better than most people. Lives in Ribley Court, Number 5. But see her first, Mr. Fane. Don't go chasing after Hicky Sharp without finding out what kind of mood he's in. I shouldn't have told you, really, but——"

" Oh, don't worry about me," said Richard. " What's the daughter's name? "

" Alice."

" How old is she? "

" Nineteen, but don't let that fool you, there isn't much she doesn't know," said Pop. " Look here, Mr. Fane, let me send a pal to find out what's doing. It won't take long. I don't like the idea of you going to Ribley Court, it's not a place for a gentleman like you."

" Pop," said Richard. " You're too old-fashioned. I'll come away with Hicky's story in my pocket and with my wallet empty. Thanks."

As he drove off he knew that Pop and Lucy were watching him from the doorway of the pub ; and their obvious anxiety made him thoughtful. He pulled up some way along the road leading to the dockside area of the Thames, and opened the dashboard pocket, looking through the oddments there; there was a small spanner. He weighed it in his hand, then put it aside, jumped out, and opened the boot of the car. In there was a length of rubber tubing, a foot and a half long. It had probably been in the car for years, and was dusty and old. He took it out, cleaned it off with a piece of rag conveniently handy, and pushed it down the side of his trousers. He twisted one end in his braces so that he could get at it easily and it wouldn't slip down, then drove towards the docks.

Here and there he passed a large car; no one was particularly surprised to see the green Alvis. The road was bordered on one side by the blank walls of big warehouses; on the other, by low walls, docks, and wharves. At places the river came in and the road ran over bridges; small ships were on either side. Few people appeared to be working. The funnels and masts of the ships, cranes, all the things that one forgot about docks when away from them, were on the river-side. He passed one ship which had an Oriental name, being unloaded by manual labour; there did not seem to be a single elevator or conveyor belt working.

Richard turned out of the dockside area after a mile or two, and pulled up at a corner where three boys were kneeling on the pavement and flicking marbles. He watched for a few moments until one dark-haired urchin looked up; he had the face and dark-brown eyes of a Chinese.

" Want sunnink? "

He had the voice of the Cockney at its nasal worst.

" That's right, soldier! Where's Ribley Court? "

The boy jerked his thumb over his shoulder, and turned back to his game. One of the others had gone on playing, and the third boy had watched him, to make sure that he didn't take advantage of being left on his own. Richard took a shilling from his pocket and spun it in the air, and the little tinkle of sound made three small heads jerk round.

" Where did you say? " asked Richard.

" Give us a ride, mister, an' we'll show yer."

" Good idea. Hop in."

" C'n I sit beside yer? "

" Sure."

The boy with the Chinese ancestry climbed in next to Richard, the others sat behind, and they rode in state, the Chinese youth giving careful and easy-to-follow instructions. Richard would have had difficulty in finding Ribley Court without them. It was a narrow turning off a narrow road, and was reached through a maze of little streets. At the corner was a shop, with fly-blown groceries in the window and a few magazines stuck in a wire holder at the doorway; each magazine cover had a picture of a blond in an advanced stage of undress.

The three guides scrambled out. Richard put the shilling back in his pocket, and three small faces fell ludicrously; so they had the manners of men, but the hearts of children. He beamed, took out half a crown and a sixpence, and spun each through the air. The Chinese lad caught both, a split second quicker than the others.

" Fair shares and no fighting over it," ordered Richard.

" Okay! "

They grinned and turned and ran off; wherever they were going to take their custom, it was not to the shop at the corner of Ribley Court.

Richard got out of the car and stood at the end of the court, liking little of what he saw. There were only

about twenty houses on each side, and it was a cul-de-sac.
The roadway was only wide enough for one car; not that
many cars would find their way into it. The front doors
opened straight on to the pavements. Two windows
were boarded up, several had broken panes, and no one
had troubled to put in weatherboards. It had a dirty,
miserable, and forlorn look; the East End of London at
its worst.

Richard strolled towards the first house; Number 1.
So Number 5 was next door but one. He looked at it
thoughtfully, and began to have second thoughts; even
the rubber piping stuck inside his trouser leg gave him
little confidence. He would have felt different if Martin
had been here. He glanced back at the Alvis—then
grinned to himself, squared his shoulders, and walked
briskly to the door of Number 5. He wasn't going to
come this far and do nothing about it. He had a vague
notion of telling the story he had already told Pop—that
he wanted to interview some of the characters of the East
End. Hicky Sharp might fall for that; vanity was the
crowning folly of most crooks, if what he had heard could
be believed. He wanted to size the man up and take his
measure. But as he knocked at the door of Number 5,
he had a nasty feeling that Barbara and Martin had the
right idea about going to the police. By now Martin
would have told his story, and the police would probably
be along soon. He felt a sneaking shame that he should
find some comfort in that.

The door was flimsy, and shook under his knock; no
one answered. He glanced at the window, and thought
that the dirty-looking lace curtain moved; it was moving,
but that might be because of the window. He knocked
again, and as he did so he saw a man out of the corner of
his eyes—a man passing the end of the street.

He put his hand to the iron knocker for a third time,
but the door opened before he touched it. He had a
swift mental picture of a small man—and the man's
hands stretched out. Before Richard realized why, and

backed away, the hand had gripped his wrist, putting on such pressure that he gasped with pain. He was pulled into the house.

The door slammed.

15

Richard felt the pain at his forearm as he was pulled forward, felt a man push past him and the grip slacken. The respite was soon over; the man grabbed his arm again and forced it behind him in a hammer lock. He was thrust along a narrow passage, past a flight of stairs which did not look wide enough to walk up, and pushed into an evil-smelling kitchen. He was frightened, confused, and helpless; yet he couldn't miss the smell, it seemed to hit him. It came from the sink in a corner; this was filled with oddments of broken crockery, tins, tea-leaves, vegetable leavings.

A small table was pushed against a narrow window. The curtain was drawn, and a single electric lamp burned high in the ceiling; not very high, for the ceiling itself was not more than seven feet. Oddments of food and crockery were at one end of the bare table, and a chair stood there; another chair was against the wall at the other end of the table.

The man pushed him towards this, let him go, gripped his shoulder, and spun him round, making him sit down. Then he backed away, to the end where the food stood, and picked up a long-bladed knife which had been sharpened so often that the blade tapered to a long whippy point.

" Who sent you? "

Richard licked his lips.

" Don't stall," the man said.

He was short and plump, and looked powerful, in spite of a round, pudgy face. Obviously he had recently shaved off a moustache; his upper lip was cleaner than the rest of his face, and he had a scar on his right cheek.

He had dark hair, now cropped close, and his hands were large and looked sinewy. He wore a navy-blue woollen sweater with a roll collar, which held his chin up, and made him look as if he were thrusting it forward aggressively. The knife, held in his right hand low by his waist, pointed upwards. He had only to lunge forward to strike Richard; and he did not look as if he would take much persuading.

A second unexpected fact forced its way into Richard's consciousness; the man had a normal speaking voice. He looked an East Ender of the vicious type, but spoke as if he had been well educated.

He moved the knife a few inches, and thrust his face forward.

" I'm speaking to you. Who sent you? Who are you? Why'd you come? "

Richard gulped.

" I—I was looking for—Hicky Sharp."

" So you were." The thin lips curled; Richard would have staked money that this was Sharp. " Why? "

" I wanted—to get a story."

" So you wanted to get a story. And now you want me to listen to it, I suppose." He swept his left hand round and slapped Richard on the side of the face. It made his head ring; it was meant to. " Let's have the truth."

" It's—true. I'm a reporter, and——"

The man stepped forward and feinted with the knife, making Richard rear backwards. He dipped his hand into Richard's pocket and drew out a wallet, emptied it over the table; a letter stuck on some butter, another fell into a jug of milk. He picked up several cards, glanced at them, then swung round with his eyes glittering.

" So you are *Fane*," he breathed. " I thought so."

Richard's head was thumping from the bang against the wall, but he was becoming aware of the rubber tubing pressing against his side. He rested his hand inside his coat, and the other appeared not to notice it.

"Well, well, so you're one of the Fanes. As if you haven't caused enough trouble! I should have known. How did you get on to me?"

"Are you—Sharp?"

"Never mind who I am, how did you get on to him? Someone squealed. Was it—*Clarke*?" The man hissed that word out, and the malice in his voice seemed to fill the room. "Was it that double-crossing swine?"

"I—I don't know. My brother——"

"Don't lie. Who squealed on Sharp?"

"I tell you I don't know."

The man drew in a hissing breath, feinted with the knife again, and slapped Richard across the face again. Richard shot out his right foot and caught him on the knee. That sent him staggering back, the knife waving in the air. Richard sprang to his feet and pulled at the rubber; it caught against his braces. He grabbed the milk jug; milk spilled over him as he flung it. Sharp ducked. The jug crashed against the wall and broke, milk splashed over Sharp's head, some trickled into his eye. He dashed his hand across his eye and leapt forward, making a sweeping blow with the knife. Richard kicked out again. The point went into his leg, he felt the searing pain, flinched, and lost his balance. He hit against the wall, and the man rushed at him, arm raised. The knife fell, but it didn't cut, it rested lightly against Richard's throat.

"Who squealed? Was it Clarke?"

Richard pressed back against the wall, standing on one leg, resting the other, the left touching lightly on the floor. He could feel blood trickling down from the cut. He was trembling, no longer with fear; he was just having difficulty in keeping his balance. The other's eyes, bloodshot and cruel, were only a foot away from him, and the sharp blade of the knife rested against his neck.

"*Was it Clarke?*"

Richard said desperately, "Yes!"

Hicky Sharp drew back, and took the knife with him. He began to speak, softly, sibilantly; he called Clarke every foul name under the sun, and went off into a stream of obscenity. What he was going to do with Clarke was nobody's business. He seemed to give himself up to fury, and Richard sidled towards the chair. He sat down, looked at his foot, and saw a little trickle of blood on the shoe and on his sock. He gritted his teeth and glanced sideways at the table. The nearest missile was a plate with some blue cheese on it, but he would have to lean right across to get it; and if he got it it wasn't going to be much use.

Sharp stopped the flood of abuse, and drew nearer again.

" Where did you see him? "

" He—telephoned."

" Saying what? "

" That—you were at Buckley Street last night."

" So he did," said Sharp. " As if he doesn't know what will happen to anyone who squeals on me. I'll fix Clarke. And I'll fix you, I——"

The door, ajar until then, opened wide. Richard saw it move out of the corner of his eye, but Sharp saw nothing. He was glaring, with the knife ready; and Richard knew that this time there would be no reprieve. He steeled himself to leap sideways. There was no need.

He heard a sneezing sound, a little louder than a normal sneeze, but not much.

Sharp didn't even turn towards the door. A bullet smacked into his temple, a strange expression distorted his face, and he toppled sideways.

．　　　．　　　．　　　．　　　．

Richard, half out of his chair, full weight on his injured leg, stared at the strangely still figure of the man on the floor, then looked towards the door. He didn't realize it, but he was holding his breath. He let it out slowly. He heard nothing else—no movement, no voices, no other shot. The silence was uncanny; just a bullet out of the blue, from a gun he'd never seen fired by a man he had never seen—and who might still be standing at the door, gun in hand.

Richard lowered himself to the floor.

After a few seconds sweat began to work out on his forehead and the back of his neck. He looked down at Sharp, who hadn't moved, whose right hand was a few inches from the brown bone handle of the knife he'd used. His legs were bent, but he had fallen on the wound, and there was only the little pool of blood on the worn linoleum near his head.

Richard got up slowly.

" Sit down," a man said abruptly.

He wasn't in sight. The voice came from the door, soft, menacing. It went through Richard like an electric shock, and he dropped back into his chair heavily. No one appeared, he could not see the man who had spoken, which meant that he was standing behind the door and looking through the tiny gap between it and the wall.

" Who are you? " the man asked.

His voice was muffled and unnatural.

" I'm a newspaperman."

" Is that so? What paper, what name? How do you know Sharp, and why did you lie about Clarke? "

Richard said slowly, " Fane." Lying was useless now, the man probably knew who he was, anyhow; and it was impossible to forget the swiftness with which death had overtaken Hicky Sharp. " *The Charade.* Sharp wanted me to blame Clark, so I——"

" Trying to tell me you lied? "

" Yes, I——"

" That's enough," came another whispering voice. " Beat it."

The voice seemed to be much farther away than that of the man at the kitchen-door. Richard hadn't suspected that a second man was there; he didn't know what the warning meant, but could guess. He flung himself downwards on his face. As he fell he heard the sneezing sound again, followed by a thud as if a bullet had hit the wall. After that was silence—and the closing of a door. He lay where he was, forehead actually touching the dead man's leg. He stayed like that for a long time, until he heard a car engine, then doors slamming, and footsteps. He tried to get up, but his leg made it difficult; there was more pain in it than there had been. He had to help himself by gripping the chair, and that meant twisting round. He was half-way up when he heard a thud at the front door, followed by a bellowed:

"Open in the name of the law!"

There was only a moment's pause before another thud shook the door violently; a second sent it crashing in. Richard was on his knees, head turned towards the door and eyes wide, when a big man came rushing in; and behind him was Martin.

．　　．　　．　　．　　．

"There's only one place for you," said Evelyn Fane some two hours later. "And that's home. Jon, we'll go back to-night and take Richard with us. They were sure there was no need to keep him in hospital, and he'll be better off in the country than in London. There'll be a chance of keeping him out of mischief, anyhow."

They were all in the Buick, pulled up at the side of a road which led into the Mile End Road, half a mile from Ribley Court. Richard was sitting next to Martin, who was at the wheel; there was comfortable room for him to stretch his bandaged leg out straight, although he hadn't been able to get into the car without help. Evelyn and Jonathan Fane sat in the back, Evelyn leaning forward and Fane sitting back with a cigarette between his lips.

They had telephoned Barbara, who was still at the office, almost as soon as Richard had been found.

Martin had come ahead in the Buick, reaching Ribley Court at the same time as a Divisional Chief Inspector of the Yard and his men. No one had been seen leaving the street; the two men must have got through the shop, the only place with a back entrance, and disappeared somewhere towards the docks. The shopkeepers had been interrogated by the Divisional Police; Martin had not been present; he had waited only long enough for his parents to arrive, and had then driven them all to the London Hospital; the police had made sure that the patient had been given immediate attention.

Richard had made a statement.

"And I hope no one is going to argue about that," Evelyn said. "We can put a bed in the morning-room, so that you won't have any stairs to climb, and you'll really give your leg a chance to mend. That's final."

Jonathan Fane looked straight ahead of him.

"Good idea," said Martin without enthusiasm.

"It's the *only* idea."

Richard turned his head. He was pale and there were bruises on his face, and Sharp's nails had scratched him on the nose. Nothing could take away his attractiveness or the impudence of his smile.

"Bless you, old lady! But until this is over I'm staying in London. By to-morrow I'll be able to get about, and——"

"Bless me, *old*——" Evelyn almost choked.

"Peace!" cried Richard. "I meant it affectionately! I know you mean it for the best, too. But it can't be done, Next time I might——"

"Next time you'll get yourself murdered!"

"Not on your life!"

"Any man in his senses, after going through what you've been through, would *want* to get out of London and take things easily for a while. Jon——" Evelyn turned to Fane, her eyes sparking. "You must make him."

"Oh, I would," said Fane, taking the cigarette from his lips. "It's the only sensible thing to do, and he knows it. There's just one difficulty."

His wife looked at him frostily.

" Of course, if you're going to *make* difficulties——"

" Not I! The police. They may want Richard to be at hand, so that they can come and ask questions. I think the best thing would be to find a hotel in London with a room on the ground floor. That'll save him the stairs. You could stay in the same hotel. If you were there you could make sure he didn't get into mischief."

Evelyn said thoughtfully, " That might be a good idea. The journey would probably overtire him, anyhow. Do you know of such a place? "

" We'll find one."

" Now that my future's been settled," said Richard lightly, " supposing we get to the office? I'll show you what stairs mean to me. Later Mother can have Scoop's room at the flat, and he can put the camp bed up in the living-room if Mother's really set on staying. Home, James."

Martin, who had not said a word during this discussion, let in the clutch.

" Mind if I drive? " he asked.

Richard grinned, but soon after they had turned into the main road and were heading west, towards the City and the West End, he was frowning. His leg was probably much more painful than he pretended, Martin decided. Richard was undoubtedly thinking about Kathleen, too— and he was soon going to get a nasty shock about Kathleen. He wouldn't like it when he heard that she had disappeared; when he knew what had been found at the Buckley Street flat his spirits would probably fall to zero. Sooner or later the news would have to be broken. There was something in the Maestro's talk of the police, too; Kelby would have a lot of questions to ask.

Martin had to slow down at the traffic lights near Whitechapel Church, and as he did so he heard a low-pitched whistle. He glanced towards the pavement. Rennie stood there, one hand in his pocket, the other held forward, finger and thumb rubbing together, and a grin on his face. He caught Martin's eye, winked, and turned away.

" Who on earth was *that*? " asked Evelyn.

Martin said, " A terrible rogue. In and out of gaol all the time, I'm told—yet one of Skip's best friends, if he only knew it. The chap who telephoned. He——"

Martin broke off and frowned. A motorist behind hooted, because the light had turned green. Martin went forward slowly, watching the way Rennie slipped among the crowd—and also watching the two uniformed policemen who were on his heels.

16

THE stairs leading to the office were shallow, and against everyone's advice Richard insisted on walking up them. He clung to the wooden rail at one side, and said that he needed no more help; but he let his father take his arm half-way up the last flight, and was white to the lips when he reached the landing. Evelyn looked at him without speaking, and that cost her a considerable effort. She led the way into the office, where Barbara was at the counter, talking to a young man and a girl in the early twenties. The family party went through, and the young man broke off, stared at Fane, nudged the girl, and said in a piercing whisper:

" There he is! "

" *Really?* " breathed the girl ecstatically.

" Go into Martin's office, will you? " asked Barbara. She glanced at Richard and frowned, but turned round to deal with the callers. She didn't spend much time on them, and they were on their way as Evelyn went into Martin's office, opening the door without looking inside, and standing aside for Richard to pass. But she was the first to see the desk, all the same. Her eyes brightened, and she turned to Martin, who was by his father's side.

" At least there's one mistake you didn't make, Scoop. Bless you, Barbara! "

Even Richard exclaimed.

Martin's desk had been cleared of papers, and a buffet meal was spread out; sandwiches, plates of cold meat, cheese, butter, biscuits, savouries—all colourful and attractive. There was even a small coffee urn, and cups and saucers. All the chairs had been brought out from the other offices, and at least two had been borrowed.

126

The upholstered client's chair was pushed against a wall, and a box stood in front of it—exactly right for Richard to rest his leg. He hobbled across to it, sat down, wiped his forehead furtively, and forced a grin.

" The miracle woman. Wish me the same luck as Scoop's had, Mother! "

" Never mind luck, have something to eat," said Evelyn. " I'm ravenous."

She filled a plate for Richard and took it across. Fane sat down, but Martin and Barbara stood up, darting here and there with oddments. For ten minutes they were busy eating and doing little talking, and the office buzzer was silent.

Barbara poured out coffee.

" This was a special favour," she said. " There's a little delicatessen shop round the corner, and the man couldn't have been more helpful."

" Probably likes brown eyes," mumbled Richard.

" What are eyes for? " asked Evelyn.

" Had many callers? "

Fane was eating brown-bread sandwiches; he had not eaten white bread for years.

" Dozens! " Barbara laughed, and blew a strand of hair away from her face. " That's an exaggeration, but there have been at least eight. I should never have believed so many would find us the first day—it's not as if we're in the telephone book. They ring up the news-papers to find out the address. The Prince is the big draw."

" Any business? "

" Darling, you don't expect miracles, do you? " Evelyn asked. " They've only just started."

" Yes." Fane smiled. " I always expect miracles."

" One or two things might develop, but they're mostly rather vague. Two more divorces, so I turned them down. I suppose I *ought* to turn them down? "

Barbara looked uncertain.

" Yes," said Fane emphatically. " You can get plenty

of business without taking up divorce work, if you go the right way about it. Neither Richard nor Martin would stand it for long, anyhow."

Martin and Richard nodded agreement, Evelyn didn't speak, but fetched Richard more coffee. All of them were conscious of constraint in the atmosphere, in spite of the concerted effort to be free and easy. Now that they were no longer hungry their thoughts turned more to the Clarke case and to murder. The buzzer kept obligingly quiet.

Fane turned to Richard.

" Skip, exactly what happened? "

" I told you when I told the police. Forget it."

" You didn't tell us why you went, how you found out Hicky Sharp's address, or "—Fane paused, smiling; all of them felt better now that the issue had been brought into the open—" whether you saw the man who shot Sharp, or are keeping something else back."

" Skip, you mustn't do that," Evelyn said. She sat next to Richard, and was looking into his face; her own expression was soft and almost pleading. " Don't do foolish things, I couldn't bear it if I thought you were always in danger."

Richard, looking much better, pressed her hand.

" No more folly! Not that kind, anyhow. Before I go crook-hunting again I want a gun. No, I didn't see him. He stood behind the door and started asking me questions, just as I told you."

" Could it have been Clarke? " asked Martin.

" Obviously. There were two of them, anyhow, one keeping watch for the police. That reminds me, how did *you* get along so soon? I was reduced to praying that the police would arrive, but I didn't expect to see Big Brother."

Martin frowned as he lit a cigarette.

" Rennie telephoned a warning. He must have been looking for Sharp himself, and saw you go in . We owe him a lot "—he smiled faintly at his mother—" Richard's best friend, remember. I'm worried about him. He was at the traffic lights at Whitechapel, and the police were after him. He told me that he did a job at Putney the night before last, and I should hate him to think I told the police about that. Can't imagine how they got on to him, though. I wonder——"

He broke off.

" Let's have it," said Fane.

" Well, if I could put a word in for him with Kelby, would it help? "

" Not at this stage." Fane was emphatic. " You don't even know if they picked him up, or if they did, why. I'd leave it. If he's in trouble, you can get legal help and do everything possible for him, and give him a hand when he comes out of gaol."

Martin didn't speak.

" We can't let the man who saved Richard's life go to prison," said Evelyn. " It's unthinkable."

" Aren't we rather getting away from the main issue? " asked Barbara, biting a chocolate biscuit. " Of course we must help Rennie in every way we can, and if we can do anything more to help catch Clarke that'll be excellent, but the chief worry at the moment is Kathleen. Rosa left just after you." Barbara drew in a deep breath, glanced at Martin, and then looked steadily into Richard's eyes. " It's no use holding out on Richard, Scoop. Kelby telephoned, soon after you'd gone, and told me what was found at Kathleen's and Rosa's flat. He wants us to tell him the moment we hear anything from either of them."

Richard stared; and everyone else looked at him. without speaking. He had lost the little colour he had regained, was in the act of lighting a cigarette, but let the lighter-cap put the flame out. His eyes were very bright; too bright, an indication of the effects of the shock and pain.

" Now what's this? "

He was gruff.

" Kathleen has disappeared—Rosa says she's been kidnapped—and thousands of pounds in forged bank-notes were found beneath the floorboards at Flat 6," Barbara said quietly. " None of the printing plates was found. Two men were arrested. They pretended to be gas fitters, sneaked into the flat, and started to get the stuff. Martin had a brainwave, and thought that someone had tried to get the girls out of the flat, so he assumed from that that someone else wanted to get in. He wondered why, and went to find out."

" Oh," said Richard. His glassy eyes turned towards his brother. " Hard on Kathleen."

" Was it? " asked Martin slowly. None of the others moved or interrupted, and he looked only at his brother. " I wondered a lot, and decided it was the best thing. If the people who hid the notes there wanted Rosa and Kathleen out of the way so that they could get them, then it suggests Rosa and Kathleen knew nothing about them. If they'd known anything, the best way of getting them out would have been to *take* them out, wouldn't it? "

Richard didn't comment.

" On the other hand, if Kathleen's mixed up in this, we might as well know now as later," Martin continued. " I don't think she is, if that opinion is worth anything. It was the only thing to do, Skip."

" Yes," said Richard slowly. " Yes, I suppose so. It's hell, though. It means that Kathleen's either on the run *or* she's——"

He didn't finish.

" Rosa used the word kidnapped, but I don't think we can take anything for granted," Barbara said briskly. " If it was simply an attempt to get the forged money out and make sure neither Kathleen nor Rosa was able to interrupt, then Kathleen will probably turn up soon—in much the way that Rosa did. I shouldn't worry too much about it."

" No," said Richard heavily.

Evelyn stood up and went across to Fane.

" Jon, Richard must rest. He'll really be ill if he stays

up much longer and starts worrying. I think we ought to take him to the Lodge, whatever he says. He can't *do* anything here. We can cancel our hotel rooms."

" Sorry. I'm staying in London."

Richard's voice held a brittle note.

" I've been thinking about that," said Barbara. " I know of a little hotel, at the back of Harrods. They've one or two ground-floor bedrooms, and I know the manager fairly well, he might be able to help. Shall I ring him? "

"Barbara," said Richard slowly, " I am really begining to envy Scoop. You are a woman of real understanding. No offence, Mother! I mean——"

Evelyn went across to him, gripped his shoulders, and pressed her cheek hard against his. When she drew back there were tears in her eyes. She put a handkerchief to her nose, sniffed, and when Fane took her arm, told him not to be ridiculous. Barbara, smiling at Martin, was already at the telephone.

·   ·   ·   ·   ·

At half-past four Richard was actually in bed at the Basil Street Hotel, and the senior Fanes were in a first-floor room, immediately above Richard's. It was a pleasant room with a double bed. Evelyn went across to it, and her eyes were gleaming.

" Yes, Barbara *has* something. I would have bet you a pound that there would be twin beds."

" Does it matter all that? " asked Fane off-handedly.

" If you don't know that I prefer a double bed after thirty years——" Evelyn began, and then saw the laughter in his eyes and the curve at his lips. She put her arms round him. " I hate you! "

" Yes, dear."

" Darling," said Evelyn a moment later, " is there anything you can do to help the boys? Over this Clarke case, I mean. I shan't feel easy until it's over. And there's this girl Richard seems to be so fond of. He must be feeling frantic. You really started the new business, it's up to you to do something."

" I didn't start any business, and I only write mysteries," Fane said mildly.

" Can't you act as you'd make the Prince act for once?" They were still standing close together, arms round each other. " That isn't too much to ask, is it? "

" Much too much! But I'll do what the Prince wouldn't do—I'll see the Assistant Commissioner at the Yard," said Fane.

" Of course! You know him, don't you? "

" We've met."

" Have a word with one of your Member of Parliament friends and tell them to talk to the Home Secretary and tell *him* to talk to the Assistant Commissioner," said Evelyn brightly. " And you tell the Assistant Commissioner that they must do something quickly. It's *miserable* for Richard."

" It wasn't very good for Mrs. Clarke," murmured Fane.

.   .   .   .   .

After his parents and Richard had left the office Martin telephoned Kelby; the Yard man wasn't in. With Barbara, Martin made notes of the various callers and their requirements; there was a widow who wanted to trace a relative believed to be in Australia; a mild-mannered woman who seemed to have a persecution complex, and was convinced that she was always being followed; and the little man who'd lost the gold watch. None of the other callers offered business other than divorce.

Martin sat back in the client's chair.

" Not exactly an impressive tally."

" My sweet, don't ask for too many miracles. When the newspapers come out to-morrow, with the story of your find at Buckley Street and Richard's trip to Ribley Court, we shall really make everyone sit up and take notice. And if we could find Clarke, or the murderer, and break up the forgery gang, we'd have a reputation that would make our fortune! Kelby can't refuse to acknowledge what you've done so far, and although he'll be annoyed with Richard, he wouldn't have heard about Hicky Sharp if it hadn't been for you. It *looks* certain Clarke killed Sharp, doesn't it? Sharp was with him at the river, was the man who collected those ashes, was probably the one man who knew that Clarke had killed his wife. So Clarke must have killed Sharp to silence the only witness."

"Whoever shot Hicky Sharp wasn't alone," Martin objected.

Barbara wrinkled her nose.

"Yes, I'd forgotten that. Try Kelby again."

Either Kelby wasn't in or he was not willing to speak to Martin. It was then nearly six o'clock, and the offices were quiet. At half-past five there had been a general exodus from the building; now only one or two people went down the stairs, one at the time.

"I suppose too much happened at once," said Barbara. "I feel horribly flat."

"So do I. Let's go somewhere or do something. Let's "—Martin grinned—"let's go and lay siege to Scotland Yard. If Kelby's there he surely can't refuse to see us. We'll threaten to tell the Press everything if he won't play ball. Coming?"

"No! Don't start high-pressuring Kelby."

"A little bit of high pressure might do him good."

"You must suppress the Richard in you," said Barbara lightly. "I—I wonder who that is?"

The telephone bell rang. As Martin lifted the receiver, the buzzer went in the outer office. They had taken it for granted that they would have no more callers to-day, and Barbara looked hopeful as she went out of the office.

A girl said to Martin, "Hold on, please, this is Scotland Yard. The Assistant Commissioner would like a word with you."

Martin whistled, called, "Bar!" and watched the

133

door hopefully, but Barbara was still in the outer office. There was a long pause, and then a man with a deep, throaty voice came on the line.

"Mr. Martin Fane? . . . This is Sir William Niven, of Scotland Yard. Can you come over here? I should like to meet you, and your father is in the office with me."

Martin made himself sound blasé. His grin was vast, and he felt a sudden buoyancy.

"I see. Yes, I *think* I can make it."

"Do, please," said Niven. "In about half an hour—good!"

He rang off, and Martin replaced the receiver, rubbed his hands together, whistled a gay little tune, and stood up. He was chuckling at the realization that his father was already trying to pull strings; no agency had ever started off with the dice loaded so heavily in its favour. He hurried to the door and heard Barbara speaking quietly; whoever it was could wait, Barbara was coming with him.

Barbara had gone into Richard's office and left the door open. Standing with her back to Martin was a girl—he guessed that she wasn't much more than a school-girl—with long hair, bedraggled and hanging over her shoulders, a short coat, woollen stockings with a hole at one heel, and down-at-heel shoes. The girl's shoulders were rounded, and she appeared to be in an attitude of utter dejection. As Martin went across Barbara looked up; her eyes told him to stay where he was. He stood still. Barbara finished speaking, and in the pause which followed he heard the girl sniff.

Then: "Dad *said* Mr. Fane would help, I just got to see him."

"Mr. Fane will do everything he can," said Barbara reassuringly. "Oh, Mr. Fane, you're back! This is Mr. Rennie's daughter, Jessica, and Mr. Rennie appears to be in some trouble with the police. He told her that he was sure you would do what you could to help."

THE girl turned round slowly, almost reluctantly, as if she could not trust the man behind her.

Martin had an impression of frightened, haunted beauty. Her face was grimy, her hair looked as if it hadn't been washed for months, but her features were delicately formed, and her eyes were almost Barbara's eyes; clear chestnut brown, fringed with lashes which curled to her cheeks and her eyebrows. She clutched the old coat over her breast. She wasn't as young as he'd thought—in the middle teens, probably, and already giving promise of a figure that would be hard to beat. Beneath the coat she wore a yellow jumper, high at the neck, taut at the front.

"You Mr. *Fane*?"

She had a whispering voice which reminded him of Rennie's hoarseness.

"Yes, Jessica." Martin went into the office. "What's happened?"

"The rozzers took my Dad. He didn't do it, I'm sure he didn't do it. He promised me he wouldn't do any more jobs, Mr. Fane, and he wouldn't break a promise to me, I'm sure about that." The words came out in a husky torrent. "He got home just before they pinched him, he told me to come here and see you, said you'd help him. Said you owed him some money, and—he said if he was sent down again I was to tell you to give it to me, so much every week, so's I couldn't lose it."

She stopped and drew a deep breath.

"Yes, I owe him some money, and I'll look after you," said Martin. "I'll try and make sure your father doesn't go inside, too. Why did they take him, do you know?"

" Once you've been inside you never get any peace from the bloody coppers." Her lips curled. " They asked him where he was on Wednesday night. *I* said he was at home, but he wasn't, and they knew *that*. Mister, you'll help him, won't you? "

" I've told you so."

" Martin," said Barbara, forgetting office formality, " apparently they live in one room, at Moor Grove, Wapping. Jessica's mother died several years ago, and she hasn't any relatives. She looks after herself if her father goes away. I don't want her to go back home until we've some news of her father—what do you think? "

" *I'll* be all right," said Jessica Rennie. " Just you look after my Dad."

" What about going to the pictures for an hour or two, and then coming to see us again? " suggested Martin. " Not here, but at my flat. And you could have a meal first."

" *Gee!* " breathed Jessica. " I'd like that, mister."

Martin gave her three half-crowns and the address of the flat at Leyden Lane.

. . . . .

" The trouble is that Rennie did do that job at Putney," said Barbara, as Martin drove in the Buick towards Scotland Yard. " There isn't much doubt about that, and I don't see that there's anything you can do if the police have discovered he was there. We could help the child, of course."

She glanced at him, but his face was set as he concentrated on driving through traffic which was gradually thinning out. The snow had stopped and the wind had dropped, but the roads were slippery and there were icy patches. A cyclist skidded towards the nearside wing, and Martin turned out and saw the cyclist's coat touch the car, but there was no damage, and the cyclist recovered his balance.

" Although I don't quite know what to do with her,"
136

said Barbara. " She told me she hates it when her father isn't at home, because of the other men in the house."

Martin took his eyes off the road for a split second.

" It's a beastly business when a child of that age has to worry about that. Apparently Rennie is a stickler for morals." Barbara wasn't being facetious. " The girl has to lock herself in her room, night and day, to avoid being pestered."

" Oh," said Martin.

" On the other hand, I don't see that you can ask Kelby anything about Rennie."

Unexpectedly Martin smiled; Barbara saw the glint of his teeth as they passed beneath a lamp in Whitehall. She made no comment, but was smiling as they passed the Cenotaph, white and ghostly in the street lights, with a few wreaths standing at its base, and two or three people grouped together on the pavement, looking at it in either reverence or curiosity. Martin glanced at it, and Barbara wondered what he was thinking. He was an idealist and a dreamer, and as sentimental as a man could be, beneath the crust of reserve which so often covered him. He would seldom give an immediate response to anything new, but liked to ponder it for hours, sometimes for days; and he seldom gave any inkling of what he thought. She was beginning to judge his likely reactions in advance; she fancied that she knew what it would be to Jessica Rennie's plight.

He went into Parliament Square, turned towards the Bridge and then the Embankment, and stopped by the other cars outside the new building. This time the sergeant at the top of the steps didn't ask him to fill in a form, but sent a constable with them to the Assistant Commissioner's office on the first floor.

Jonathan Fane was sitting near the desk, in an arm-chair, smoking a pipe and looking as if he owned the place. Kelby, on an upright chair, had nothing like the same look of confidence. Sir William Niven, a tall, angular man with high cheek-bones and a long jaw—as long, almost, as Sergeant Wimple's—sat behind a large flat-topped desk. His grey hair was plastered down over a large head, his eyes seemed to be hooded by wrinkled lids, and he had bushy eyebrows and a small mouth. His cheeks were so red near the bones that it looked almost as if he used rouge.

He stood up.

" Ah. Good evening, Mr. Fane."

He came round the desk and shook hands.

" Good evening, Sir William. This is Miss Marrison, my fiancée."

" And secretary, I understand. Or is it partner? " Niven spoke briskly, as if anxious to waste no time in formalities. " Glad to see you both. Been hearing a great deal about you. Sit down, sit down." There were two more arm-chairs. " Your father is worried, naturally, about this case. Unpleasant case. Remarkable coincidence that you have become involved—you might call it lucky! " He gave a quick smile, and showed a lot of teeth. " You've been very helpful—eh, Superintendent? "

" Very," said Kelby, and took as long to utter the one word as Niven needed for a whole sentence.

" Yes. So we want to be helpful. And frank. We have no news of Miss Wilder. And Miss Rosa Harding seems to have gone away without leaving an address, but apparently of her own free will. She has taken only a few clothes, so presumably she will be returning to Buckley Street. No reason why she shouldn't go away, of course. And she was questioned before she went. Know Miss Harding well? "

" I've only seen her twice," said Martin.

" I see. Miss Wilder told you much about her? "

" No."

" Well, Kelby has seen her. She says that she knows nothing more about Miss Kathleen Wilder than she has already told us—or told you, rather. Ah. We have not yet informed her of what we found at the flat. Obvious possibility that she knew something about it. Miss Wilder, too."

Martin nodded impassively.

"Now, other things. Put me right if I go wrong, Kelby." Niven gave the quick, toothy smile again. "We feel that you have earned unusual confidences. Thanks to you we know that two men, one of them Hicky Sharp, put Mrs. Clarke's body in the river at Putney. No doubt that Hicky Sharp was there, none at all—found his prints. Can't be sure of the other man, more's the pity—no finger-prints, nothing to guide us at all. However, we've got to Sharp. And, as you know, he was murdered." In spite of the " as you know " Niven was talking almost as if he were giving them information which they hadn't known before, and was bestowing a great favour. " Now! Those notes were hidden in Miss Wilder's flat—it is her flat, she has the tenancy. Obviously possible that she knew, as we've said. Just possible that Clarke—no doubt that Clarke is involved and made the paper on which the notes were printed, he's been making it over many years, never enough to notice, always enough to flood the market with spurious notes—ah! Just possible, as I say, that he obtained a key to Number Six and, when the two tenants were out, went in and hid the notes under the floorboards. He would then feel safe, should he be suspected and his own rooms be searched. One great obstacle—see it? " he flashed.

Martin didn't hesitate.

" Oh, yes. The difficulty he'd have in getting the notes back unless he could get in and out of Miss Wilder's flat when he liked. A key would only serve part of the purpose. He'd need to be sure the two girls were out long enough for him to take up the floorboards and the carpet. So while it would be a fairly safe place, it wouldn't be convenient."

" Exactly. Suggests that one or the other of the young women might know something about it. Now the evidence we have so far is that Miss Wilder told you about the strangeness of Clarke's manner over the dog. If she were conspiring with Clarke, you would expect her to keep quiet. Eh? "

" Yes."

" There is the problem," said Niven. " One other thing—put me right if I go wrong, Superintendent—and that is, the two men we caught. Gas fitters! No shadow of doubt about their guilt. They admit that they were working for Hicky Sharp. He told them to go and get the notes, told them where they would be. At the time of their statement they didn't know that Sharp had been murdered. Couldn't know "—the grin flashed—" because he hadn't been murdered. So our problem is to find the man who murdered Sharp. Probably it's Clarke—eh, Superintendent? "

" I shall be surprised if it isn't," said Kelby. " Excuse me, Sir William, but Mr. Fane and Miss Marrison do understand this is in confidence, don't they? "

" Eh? Of course."

Martin nodded, Barbara echoed:

" Of course."

" Naturally! Thing is, we think you might be able to help us. Quickest way of seeing the business over is to catch the killer. Ah! Possibility that Miss Harding or Miss Wilder can tell us something about it is quite obvious. We should like you to find out what you can about Miss Harding. Perhaps you can find out where she may have gone, and continue to meet her socially. You could help us here. I don't want her to think she is under police surveillance—Miss Harding is like many young women, she freezes up at the sight of a detective. Doesn't necessarily mean a guilty conscience, either. Could be very useful. Don't you agree, Superintendent? "

Kelby said, " Yes, I do," so slowly that it obviously went against the grain. " But there's a question you haven't asked Mr. Fane yet. How did he get on to Hicky Sharp? Who tipped him off? Was it Rennie? "

MARTIN sat back in his chair and took out his cigarette-case—a sure indication to Barbara and his father that he was stalling, and couldn't make up his mind whether to tell the truth. In fact, he was trying to decide whether the truth would help in the search for the murderer, which really meant the search for Clarke, or whether any harm done to Rennie would be pointless.

" Ah," said Niven. " Yes. Was it, Mr. Fane? "

" What makes you think it might have been anyone named Rennie? " asked Martin.

Niven waved to Kelby.

" We know it was somone who told you he was doing a job by the river at Putney, Mr. Fane. We gave a lot of attention to that job. A house was broken into. Clothes, food, and money were taken. Loose money only. Valuables were left untouched, although they could easily have been stolen, and all the clothes were women's clothes. We've had Rennie inside several times for doing jobs like that—he never takes a great deal."

" Oh," said Martin. " Not a really bad man."

" There are a lot worse than Rennie," said Kelby bluntly. " The man's a fool. If he would get a steady job he could live comfortably. He idolizes his daughter, and she tries to keep him straight. The trouble is that she can't read or write properly, and can't get a job because of it."

" Can't read or write! " exclaimed Barbara.

" It's not so rare as you think," said Kelby. " A lot of youngsters in the East End never get any real schooling, their parents keep them away on one excuse or another, and make them work. Greed usually. That wasn't the case with Rennie's girl. The mother was an invalid for years. Rennie and the girl nursed her. He idolized his wife, and she died when he believed proper medical attention could have saved her. That made him bitter. He was always on the fringe of crime, was one of the out-of-works for years. Then he started stealing to pay bills. Now he uses the excuse that as he has a record he can't get a job. In fact he could, but——"

Jonathan Fane intervened mildly:

" At a slave wage, I expect. Aren't you astonished how often people want to employ ex-convicts and give them another chance, and pay them so badly that they really kick them into more roguery? "

Kelby didn't answer.

" Has been known," said Niven.

" Has been known my foot! " Fane sat up and became almost aggressive. " It's constantly happening. I've had a dozen old lags come to see me, they've all told me the same story, and I've checked. Even friends of mine seem to think that by giving an old lag a job that will just keep him from starvation they've done their duty. I rather like the sound of this Rennie."

" Apparently your son does, too," Kelby said nastily.

Martin said, " I haven't said a thing about Rennie. In any case, all I could give you would be hearsay evidence. Have you picked him up? "

" Yes."

" Has he admitted anything? "

" No. But he had four pound notes, probably taken from the house the other night——"

" Oh, were they? " said Martin. " Can you prove it? "

" No, but——"

" Have you found the clothes that were stolen? "

Kelby looked down his nose.

" Yes."

" At Rennie's home? "

" No," said Kelby, and looked up, his gaze very steady.

142

" At a Mission, where they hand out clothes to the poor who need them. We've known Rennie steal a whole wardrobe and hand most of the stuff over. He only takes enough money to keep himself going, food—which I think he uses himself, but he always gets rid of tins and packing, so that it can't be traced—and often clothes. I've told you that Rennie isn't one of the worst. We've no desire to persecute him. But if he saw Hicky Sharp at Putney he might have seen something else we can use. And we want Clarke."

" I see," said Martin heavily.

He was conscious of his father's and Barbara's gaze, and was pretty sure what they were trying to say, that in the circumstances he would have to name Rennie. Kelby was right, too; the police might get something more out of the little man who could laugh at himself. He didn't like it, but if it would lead to the murderer——

He sat up.

" Can I have a few minutes' talk with Rennie alone? "

Kelby frowned but didn't speak.

" Why? " asked Niven quickly.

" Afterwards I should be able to say whether he's the man who gave me the information," said Martin blandly.

Kelby said, " He was the man, and we know it, but we can't break him down yet. If you confirm, we can make him talk all right, and once he's admitted he was at Putney we'd get everything else out of him. If you're worried about what he'll get, we could probably make sure it won't be more than six months."

" Can I have a word with him? " Martin asked patiently.

His father was smiling with deep satisfaction.

It took them ten minutes to make up their minds; then they decided to let Martin go and talk to Rennie in the remand cell at Cannon Row police-station, which was only a stone's throw from the Yard.

. . . . . .

Rennie was lying on his back on a mattress placed on

wooden boards standing on trestles close to the wall of a small cell. There were one or two oddments of plain wooden furniture; a chair, a table, and a small bookcase, with half a dozen books in it, each of which looked as if it were old enough to go on the shelves of a Public Library. The cell was barred on one side, the walls were blank, except for a small barred window.

Rennie's knees were bent upwards, and his head rested on his hands. His hair was an untidy grey-black mop. He heard the keys rattle as a sergeant opened the door, but didn't look up. Martin stepped inside, and the door was locked on him; Rennie maintained the pose of indifference. Martin went across, pulled up the chair, and sat down, so that the man had only to glance sideways to recognize him. It was a long time before Rennie glanced sideways; when he did he straightened his legs and sat up like a Jack-in-the-box.

" Strike a light! " he breathed.

" Hallo," said Martin. " Cigarette? "

He offered his case.

" I'll tell O'Reilly," breathed Rennie, and took a cigarette; the white paper made the dirt beneath his nails look black. He was exactly as Martin had seen him before, except that he had washed his face, and the yellow matter was gone from his eyes and mouth. " So you've the nerve to come an' see me, *Mister* Fane."

" That's right."

" After you squealed——"

" Don't be a fool, Rennie, and keep your voice down, if you don't want everyone to hear. I haven't named you. You left your trade-mark at Putney, and they took a chance. They want to question you about the two men you saw, they think you might be able to give them more information."

Rennie looked at him uncertainly.

" I named *H*icky, didn't I? "

" It's not enough."

" You've got me into a narsty mess, you 'ave."

" That's right," said Martin dryly. " I went to Putney, I broke into the house, I gave the clothes to the Mission— blame me."

His eyes gleamed.

An answering smile appeared in Rennie's.

" Out wiv it, guv'nor. Wot do yer want me to do? "

" Tell Kelby you were in Putney, walking along the river, and saw these men. Tell him you knew that if you reported to the police they'd take it for granted you'd been burgling nearby, so you passed on the information without getting yourself into trouble."

Rennie's eyes were smiling more freely.

" Listen, guv'nor," he said sorrowfully, " you're young, you've a lot to learn. The dicks don't take any notice of that kind of spiel. When I tell them I was at Putney I can kiss my 'and to my own front door for twelve months. Might get more this time. You mean well, guv'nor, but you ought to open a shop, not play arahnd detecting." He swung his legs off the bed. " That fifteen quid—not backing aht, are you? "

" It's yours."

" Give it to my kid. I told her to come and see you, but she'll be too scared, I bet. Ten bob a week, that'll last thirty weeks, and I might be aht by then. That a bargain? "

" Tell Kelby what I've told you, and I'll make it a pound a week until you come out," said Martin. " Plus her wages."

Rennie looked startled, then suspicious.

" Wages for what? "

" Working at the office. We need a girl to be polite to callers and ask them to wait, answer the telephone and do odd jobs. Reading and writing will come in time. Miss Marrison—my fiancée, you saw her this morning—will see that Jessica's all right."

Rennie rubbed his nose slowly, and there was a gleam in his eyes which now showed no hint of suspicion.

" Where's Kelby? "

Martin stood up.

"That's fine, Rennie. And listen—don't make any admission. You were just walking along the river-side. You might have broken into a place, if you hadn't seen these two men and you thought it was too hot for you. As it was, you scrammed. Don't admit anything, understand? Kelby might be persuaded to believe you."

"Not on your life," said Rennie. "But if you'll give Jessica a job, it'll be worth a oner. Listen, think you could get 'er into a girls' 'ostel, or sunnink? That place where we live isn't fit for a pig, never mind a good girl like my Jessica."

"We'll fix something," Martin promised.

.   .   .   .   .

Half an hour later Kelby actually went down to the front hall with Barbara and the two Fanes, and was affability itself. He reminded Martin to be discreet when dealing with Rosa Harding. There was no reason to think she was involved, beyond what they already knew. Kelby stood on the top step of the Yard, with the others grouped round him, shook hands, and said:

"Take it very easy, Mr. Fane. These people are killers. If you get a line let me know. Don't repeat the mistake your brother made. You'll be surprised how much easier your business will be if we get along well together, and I like the way you've started."

Martin smiled faintly.

"Thanks. Go easy with Rennie, won't you?"

"We'll hold him to-night, and if nothing else turns up he'll be released in the morning—we won't put him on charge. We can't *prove* he did those jobs, you know. The magistrate would probably say the case was proved, but it has to be put to him first, hasn't it? I don't dislike Rennie. But don't forget, he *might* know more than he says."

Martin frowned. "How?"

"Work it out for yourself!" Kelby was breezy.

146

" Now I must go and have a talk with him. Good night! "

. . . . .

A doctor had given Richard a sedative, and he was already too sleepy to talk. Evelyn Fane crept out of his room just after eight o'clock, went to the entrance hall, and looked along the street, in the hope that Jonathan was coming back; he wasn't in sight. She went into the lounge, where three elderly men were reading newspapers and two elderly women were talking in hushed tones, sat down and looked through a copy of an illustrated weekly, and automatically glanced down the book page. She smiled when she saw a review of the latest story of the Prince; a slightly patronizing notice of the kind that usually annoyed her much more than it did Jonathan. She tucked the magazine under her arm and went upstairs.

Jonathan hadn't returned by half-past eight.

She strolled down to the street again, saw a pale-coloured car, thought it was the Buick—and was disappointed. She shivered, because it was cold although the wind had dropped, and went back into the warmth of the hall. She started for the stairs, changed her mind, and went to Richard's room. It was approached along a narrow passage—there were two rooms opposite each other, quiet and secluded; the window of Richard's room overlooked a narrow alley which led from Lasil Street to a main road.

She turned the handle slowly and pushed. The door didn't open. She frowned and pushed harder. The door moved a little, but something was stopping it from opening. It hadn't jammed when she had opened it earlier, and she had done so several times. She put her shoulder to it and pushed harder, without any luck. She didn't want to make too much noise, in case Richard was asleep. She turned away, and as she reached the hall Jonathan and Barbara came in.

Her eyes lit up.

147

"Sorry we're late." Fane kissed her lightly; he usually kissed her, however short a time they'd been parted. "We were kept at the Yard, but everyone is being very helpful—the boys are in favour!"

"That's something," Evelyn conceded. "Where's Martin?"

"He's gone to look for this Rosa Harding woman."

"Rosa Harding? Oh, that creature who came into the office this morning," said Evelyn scornfully. "I wouldn't trust him with her, Bar, if I were you. I wouldn't trust her with anyone in long trousers. What does he want to see her for?"

"Hunting for clues," smiled Fane.

"I'll bet you put him up to that," said Evelyn. "Jon, I'm a bit puzzled. I can't get into Richard's room. He was sleepy, and he'd had a little steamed fish for dinner— I haven't had mine yet, by the way—and I left him. Now the door's stuck."

"If he's asleep, why disturb him?" asked Fane.

"I'd just like to see that he's comfortable. If he's asleep it will take a lot to wake him."

"I'll see if I can open the door."

Fane went along, with the women following him, talking in under-tones. He stood at the door and did exactly what his wife had done, but his reaction wasn't quite the same. He pushed very hard, studied the door as it moved, then stood back and frowned; but he didn't say why.

"I don't want to disturb him," he said. "You go into dinner—or do you want a wash first?"

"Barbara probably does."

"Well, go upstairs, and I'll be along soon," said Fane. He went with them as far as the hall, watched them out of sight up the stairs, then went back to Richard's door. He pushed at the top; the door moved. He pushed at the bottom; it didn't move at all—nor was there any give at the side near the lock.

"That's bolted at the bottom and locked," he said

aloud, and hurried back to the hall. A porter, short, wizened, and dressed in a shabby uniform, was standing by the reception desk. " Come with me, will you? "

" Yes, sir? "

" Isn't my son's window just round the corner? "

" Down the alley, sir, that's right."

" Show me the way, will you? " Fane's manner obviously impressed the porter, who led the way to the door and held it open. They hurried out, Fane wrapping his coat more tightly about him, turned along the alley, and reached the window. It was open a foot or more at the bottom.

" That's unusual, sir, for this cold weather," said the porter. " Wouldn't think he'd be too hot to-night, would you? "

" No, I wouldn't." Fane pushed the window farther up, and it squeaked noisily. The room itself was in darkness, and only faint light came from either end of the alley. " Isn't there usually a light somewhere here? "

" Come to think of it, there *is*."

" I don't like this," Fane said, as much to himself as to the porter. " You're thinner than I am. Climb in, will you? "

" Yes, sir. What do you think——"

" I don't know what to think," said Fane. " Get in and put on the light, please. Don't touch anything— the door, bed, anything. Understand? "

" Yes, sir."

The porter climbed through, banged his head on the window and swore mildly, then disappeared towards the door, which was just visible as a white blur; so was the bed. A moment later the light went on, and Fane narrowed his eyes against the glare. Next moment he looked towards the bed.

It was empty.

JONATHAN FANE hurried round to the front of the hotel, followed by the porter, who summoned the manager, a round-eyed, round-faced man with a permanently worried look. He came towards Fane, puzzled but not yet alarmed. He frowned when he saw Fane's expression; Fane's eyes had unaccustomed hardness, his lips were compressed.

"This is rather surprising, sir, I understood that your son couldn't get about very easily. I haven't seen him, but——"

"He couldn't get about. Let me use your telephone, will you? In the office. And say nothing about this, please." Fane was bleakly brisk as he looked at the porter and the receptionist; they nodded a promise of discretion. The manager led the way to his office; it was office-cum-sitting-room, and his plump and untroubled-looking wife was in an easy-chair, listening to a Brahms concerto. "Sorry to worry you," said Fane.

"There's the telephone."

The manager pointed to a corner where the telephone kept a needlework basket company.

"I'll turn the radio down, dear," said his wife.

"Thank you." Fane went to the telephone, dialled Whitehall 1212 and asked for Kelby; the manager and his wife exchanged startled glances at the "Superintendent". "Yes, I'll hold on," said Fane. While he waited he stared at a small picture over the fireplace, where a coal fire burned brightly. He seemed to be waiting a long time before Kelby came on the line. "Hallo, Kelby. Jonathan Fane again. More trouble, and it's serious."

"Sorry about that. What is it?"

Fane now looked straight at the manager.

"My son Richard was at the Lasil Street Hotel, with a ground-floor room and a window overlooking an alley. The door is locked and bolted—I haven't touched it. The window is open, and Richard has disappeared. I don't believe he would have left by himself. He was sleeping under a drug, and even if he'd been wide awake I can't imagine that he would have gone out to-night. He could hardly hobble about on that injured leg."

Kelby said, "I *see*. I'll send a squad."

"Thanks. I'll be upstairs," said Fane. He put the receiver down, and the manager and his wife stood as they might in a tableau. Fane said, "I'm afraid he was taken out, but you can rely on the police being as discreet as possible. Sorry about it."

He turned and went out, but hesitated in the hall; and Barbara came down the stairs, smiling. She looked delightful in a dark-blue dress, freshly made up, dark hair brushed and combed.

"Hallo, Maestro! Mother's gone ahead, she was so hungry."

"Oh." Fane frowned, and Barbara's smile disappeared. "Get her, will you, and bring her upstairs. Richard's missing."

Barbara caught her breath.

She touched Fane's hand then, and hurried towards the dining-room, while he went slowly upstairs. He wasn't worried about the need for telling Evelyn; she would take this well, she always took big troubles well, however bad they might be; only trifles annoyed and irritated her. Evelyn would stand still and look at him with fear clouding her eyes, and it would be an echo of the fear that he felt for Richard.

The unknown man who had killed Hicky Sharp had tried to kill Richard.

Would anyone else have any reason for kidnapping him?

.   .   .   .   .

A Flying Squad car was on the spot in ten minutes. Before the men had finished their examination of the room, door, and window for finger-prints, Kelby arrived. They found nothing to help them.

. . . . .

Martin whistled softly to himself as he drove away from the Licker Club, in Soho. He had never been there before, and did not want to go there again. Although early, and London club life had not really started, the Licker Club had been filled with hangers-on of the screen, stage, and newspaper world. Here, in a kind of bedevilled half-light, all the disappointed people on the fringes of the professions, and many of the hopeful but ill-advised beginners, bandied about the Christian names of stars and people that mattered, and lived in a never-never land of unfulfilled promises and futile boasting. From here Richard picked up some of his gossip for *Charade*. Martin recalled with satisfaction that Richard said he always left the Licker with a sigh of relief.

Rosa was a member.

Richard had told Martin that last night, on the way home. He had told him—defensively, of course—that Kathleen had been a member, but had shown the good sense to stop coming and not to continue with her membership. Kathleen still had hopes, Rosa had none. Rosa was well known in the screen and stage world as a has-been; she was thirty-five. Her face wasn't photogenic, and her figure was top-heavy—too top-heavy even for the chorus. She had never been an able actress, but had hammed a few parts before her ambitions had overcome what little histrionic ability she was ever likely to have.

From one of her friends, who had been prepared to tell her own life story for a couple of pink gins, Martin had now learned where he would probably find Rosa, unless she had run away or been kidnapped. She would be with her paramour, Wilfred Henderson, of The Beams,

Common Rise, Wimbledon. He was believed to be wealthy, and he certainly put some financial backing into second-feature British films, and into documentaries. If Rosa's friend could be believed, he was one of the few " small " men in British films who made money out of his investments, chiefly because he made sure that the film companies he backed economized rigidly on every item. He remained popular, because the results meant that he could give steady work to a number of small-part players.

He'd first met Rosa, the friend said, when she had gone for a photogenic test. He'd turned her down for the films—he had a " nose " for good performers, but—well, Martin knew how it was, didn't he? The friend had quickly reached Christian-name terms. Henderson had fallen for Rosa, and Rosa had fallen for his bank account. She often spent week-ends at The Beams, and had even talked of marriage, although she, the friend, thought that was all my-eye-and-Betty-Martin, Wilfie wasn't the marrying kind. Oh, no, he wasn't married. According to Rosa he had a manservant and two gardeners. Apart from that there was little she could say, except one thing— Wilfie was loyal. He had been loyal and, as far as was known, faithful to Rosa for nearly six months. In fact Rosa would have been in a very poor plight without him.

Wilfie seldom came to the Licker Club these days.

Martin, whistling to himself, turned all this over in his mind as he drove towards Wimbledon. His way took him over Putney Bridge, looking right; not far along there, Mrs. Clarke had been dumped into the Thames. That set him thinking about Rennie and Jessica—he must get to Leyden Lane in time to see Jessica; if she arrived and found no one at the flat she would probably think he and Barbara had let her down. Jessica probably felt that few people had good intentions. It was an odd set-up. Rennie was a character, in his way—and Kelby certainly didn't think too badly of him. The man apparently had a kind of Robin Hood complex, a distorted outlook but not a vicious one. A man like Rennie would be an invaluable contact in the East End for—anyone.

Even for Prince.

Martin grinned broadly. Prince, in his father's uninhibited imagination, had a dozen such contacts as Rennie.

He reached Wimbledon, drove along the Common road, and stopped by a policeman who directed him to The Beams. He wondered why the house had been given that name, shrugged the question aside, and caught sight of the name, written in white on black gates, on the right-hand side of a wide road. Here all the houses stood in their own grounds. Common Rise was near the large, partly wooded stretch of commonland, chief recreation centre for countless thousands of West and South-west Londoners. It was one of the best residential parts of London, although not the most fashionable. Most of the houses had been built in sombre Victorian days, and made up in solidity for what they lacked in architectural beauty.

Martin swung the Buick into a circular drive. A light burned over the front door of the house, and from what he could judge this wasn't a Victorian horror; it was low-built and long. The headlights caught the oak beams in the front wall; so one question was answered. The lights also showed up the trim lawns and the flower-beds; in one a mass of daffodils were already flowering. Martin pulled up outside the front door and considered his approach. Rosa might be annoyed because he had come to the love-nest, might refuse to see him. He thought he could handle that situation.

A manservant dressed in black opened the door.

" Good evening, sir."

" Good evening. Is Miss Harding in? "

" I will find out, sir, if you will be good enough to give me your name."

The manservant, who spoke like a automaton, stood aside for Martin to pass. He was a film servant; they didn't exist in real life. He had a pale face, winged collar, and grey tie, and his dark hair was brushed sleekly over a small head. He bowed as if he had been trained to the genuflection since his youth.

" Martin Fane," said Martin. " Tell her that it is about Miss Wilder, will you? "

" I will find out if she is *in*, sir."

The man turned towards the stairs and went up, without glancing round. Martin looked about a spacious hall, panelled in oak, with parquet floor, skin rugs, and a few old-fashioned firearms on the walls. It was a gem of a hall, and the furniture must have cost a fortune. Across the ceiling were two great beams; they looked genuinely old. He could spend half an hour looking round this little collection.

The manservant appeared at the head of the stairs, his impassive face giving nothing away. He did not speak until he was a couple of yards away from Martin. Then his words were uttered in the same measured way.

" Mr. Henderson will see you, sir."

" Mr. Henderson——"

" Yes, sir, if you will be good enough to follow me," said the manservant, and turned and marched up the stairs again with practised precision.

Martin followed, and heard a woman speak. Rosa was here; presumably Rosa was claiming her Wilfred's protection.

ROSA was sitting in an arm-chair by the side of a small, bow-shaped desk. She was dressed in a scarlet dinner-gown, cut so low at the front that it left practically nothing to the imagination. She was well made up, and her hair was piled on top of her head, Edwardian fashion; it added to the length of her face and made her even more striking than when he had last seen her. There was beauty in her, of a kind; but she was too overpowering in appearance and manner; there was a stridency about her which most people would dislike.

Wilfred Henderson sat behind the desk. Rosa's forceful personality and impressive appearance made him seem a little nondescript podge of a man. He wasn't fat, although his dinner-jacket was a trifle too tight. He wasn't unlike Hicky Sharp to look at, although he had more definite features and an air of well-being that Hicky certainly hadn't shown to Richard. He was bigger, too. In fact, he exuded goodwill and well-being. His face was set in a smile which creased his cheeks, he had a lot of large teeth, probably false, and his scanty hair was still black— or dyed—and smoothed down over his head; streaks of pink showed through from his cranium.

He stood up.

" What the devil do you mean by following me here? " demanded Rosa angrily; her colour wasn't all rouge.

" Now, my sweet——" began Henderson.

" It's a damned outrage, that's what it is."

" Now, my sweet." Henderson had an unexpectedly deep voice. " Don't spoil a wonderful evening by quarrelling with Mr. Fane. I'm sure he has the best of intentions."

" Best of intentions," sneered Rosa.

" Do sit down, Mr. Fane," said Henderson, and offered his hand. It looked flabby, but was firm. " I am afraid both of us are rather excited to-night, I hope you'll forgive us. Miss Harding——"

" Why did you follow me here? " demanded Rosa.

Martin smiled as if she had welcomed him as amiably as Henderson.

" I hate worrying you, Miss Harding, but I'm so worried about Kathleen. She——"

" *You* are? I'm not surprised," said Rosa, and sarcasm dripped from her tongue. " I always warned her that Richard Fane wouldn't do her any good, he's a pampered young fool. He even has to get his brother to chase around looking for his girl friends. If he were a *man*——"

" He's had a nasty accident. He won't be able to get about for a bit, and there's nothing else he can do. He met the accident looking for Kathleen."

" Oh, dear," said Henderson.

Rosa didn't speak, but bit her lips; then she had the grace to stand up and come across to Martin, smiling; and he remembered the remarkable change in her manner at the flat, when she had realized that something was wrong apart from Ching's misadventure.

" I'm sorry, Mr. Fane. That was unkind of me. I hope Richard isn't badly hurt."

" Not seriously, but it's a nasty leg wound. Consequently I feel that I must do everything I can to find Kathleen. The police haven't had any luck. I could have worried them more, of course, in fact I understood that one of them was coming to see you, and—I wanted to get in first. I had some trouble finding out where you were, but a friend at the Licker Club suggested that you might be here."

Rosa went back to her chair; and her eyes were narrowed, hiding much of their brilliance.

" I don't know that I can do a thing. The police— I've seen them once. What else do they want? "

"Oh, have you seen them?" Martin looked crest-fallen. "Then I'm too late—you'll have told them everything you know about the man you met at Picca-dilly Circus."

"Everything," affirmed Rosa.

"Well, that's a blow. I thought perhaps there might be something you'd overlooked when you came to my office. I don't mind what I do to try to find Kathleen. Didn't he give you *any* idea where she might be?"

"None at all." Rosa was vehement. "I tried to make him, but he frightened me. He was a complete stranger. I suppose I should have gone to the police at once, but I thought it better to come to you."

"Oh, it was. I'm grateful. Er—I suppose Kathleen hasn't had any trouble lately. Before all this blew up, I mean?"

"Not to my knowledge," said Rosa.

Martin lapsed into silence, and Henderson pushed a box of cigarettes across the desk. The silence was broken by the scraping of a match. Rosa held out her hand for a cigarette, Henderson apologized profusely for not offering her one, jumped up, and lit it for her. She let smoke trickle through her nostrils, and looked at Martin with her eyes half-closed. He was not at all sure that Rosa had told him everything that she knew. He wasn't sure, either, that he was the right man to tackle her. She was deep; and his mother, who was a good judge, didn't trust her. He didn't trust her himself.

"It's very distressing," said Henderson. "I only wish there were something I could do to help. As it is, I'm grateful in *one* way." He squeezed Rosa's shoulder lightly. "Crisis often leads to decision, Mr. Fane, you've probably noticed that before. I heard about Rosa's distress and anxiety, and decided that it was wrong that she should live on her own—or more or less on her own. It's not a good thing, and—you are the first to know, Mr. Fane! Forgive me for being so full of it—we are going to be married."

158

Rosa was smiling thinly.

"Oh," said Martin weakly. "Congratulations, Mr. Henderson. My best wishes, Miss Harding. Well, you won't want me to stay any longer." He stood up. "If there's anything at all you remember that might help, you will tell me, won't you?"

"Gladly, gladly," Henderson answered for Rosa.

"Thanks. Er—will you be returning to Buckley Street? No business of mine," Martin added, and looked rather foolish, "but if we do find Kathleen soon, she won't want to stay at the flat by herself."

"My fiancée is *not* to return there, I have been most definite." Henderson showed himself as a man of decision. "The unhappy, not to say grisly, emotions which must follow living opposite a place where such a horror took place—I needn't say more."

"What about poor old Ching?"

"Ching is already here," said Rosa. She stood up again and held out her hand. "I'm terribly sorry about Kathleen, I do hope you find her. I'll *never* be able to rest until she's found."

"I'm sure," said Martin. "Thank you. Good night."

Henderson showed him to the front door, with the dark-clad manservant standing in the background.

. . . . .

Martin hadn't trusted Rosa before, and trusted her much less now. The swift change in her manner suggested only one thing; that she was acting all the time, and could switch her mood at will. He had a strong feeling, amounting almost to conviction, that she knew much more than she had admitted. She was a cold-hearted shrew with an eye for the main chance, and she had used the murder and Kathleen's disappearance to screw Henderson up to popping the question. Nice for Rosa.

Martin drove off slowly, thoughtfully.

He hadn't come out of that interview well. He had sounded foolish, and felt foolish most of the time. Actually

159

confronting someone like that, slanting his questions to prise out information they didn't want to give, was a new and not pleasant experience. He had a feeling that Rosa had made a complete fool of him, had been laughing at him all the time. Kelby was right; there were some jobs which the Yard did much better. He hadn't learned anything new. And he had been clumsy. Sir William Niven had suggested meeting Rosa socially, and he had just barged in.

He was not making a good beginning as a detective. He smiled wryly as he drove towards Putney and London. This was reaction, of course, and he would get over it; but when he really faced facts, he and the agency would have done little or nothing but for Rennie's intervention.

That led him to consider Kelby's cryptic remark—that Rennie might know more than he had pretended. Martin couldn't see how. Rennie had run a great risk in coming to see him. He'd come to cash in on what he knew of the incident on the jetty. There wasn't any other likely explanation.

Martin whistled suddenly, and his eyes hardened.

There was another; Kelby had seen it from the beginning, he was hours behind. Supposing Rennie worked *with* Clarke. Supposing Clarke had wanted Hicky Sharp to be caught. He would have wanted someone to squeal; Rennie was as good as a squealer as anyone else. In short, Rennie might have been employed to betray Hicky Sharp. Kelby was on to that all right. There would still be one thing unexplained, though; if the plot demanded that Hicky Sharp should be betrayed, why *kill* Sharp?

What was the most likely reason for killing him?

There were two possibilities. One was that he had tried to get the counterfeit money from the Buckley Street flat for himself, Clarke had discovered that, and killed him. The other was that the police had been after Sharp, and Clarke had killed him to make sure he didn't talk.

Martin looked at the dashboard clock, which was twenty minutes slow; it was nine o'clock. Jessica would probably be at Leyden Lane by now, and it wasn't likely that Barbara would go there until he returned. The best thing would be to go straight to his own flat. He could call Barbara from there.

He went over everything that Jessica and Rennie had said. Rennie had undoubtedly been convincing, it was hard to believe that he had lied. That was one advantage which Kelby had over Martin; Kelby started out by distrusting anything which a man of Rennie's stamp said. It was an inevitable police attitude. He, Martin, was too easily persuaded to take a man at his face value. By sending Jessica to the office Rennie had worked on his emotions; that had probably been deliberate.

Martin began to feel that everyone concerned was making a fool of him. Kelby was patronizing when he wasn't hostile. Rennie was playing him for a fool. Jessica, in spite of the attractiveness of the *gamine*, was helping her father. Rosa laughed at him openly. Martin even had a feeling that his father was as much amused as anything else by the venture. That was probably unjust, but he was in a mood to think that everyone was either tolerant or patronizing. This was a daydream, they thought; better let him dream for a while, he would come down to earth soon enough.

He was no nearer finding Kathleen; and Kathleen mattered. He would have felt a kind of responsibility for her even without Richard's personal interest. He wished he knew for certain how Richard felt about her; it was too easy to assume that he knew that. Richard was deeper than a lot of people admitted.

He reached the West End, which seemed busier than usual, drove to Leyden Lane and put the car on the waste patch near by, slipped the key into his pocket, and soon looked up at the window of the flat. It was in darkness, of course—no one was likely to be there. No one was walking up and down or standing about in the narrow lane itself. The only lights were from the street-lamps and the windows of a restaurant a little way from the grocery shop.

He opened the street door and stepped inside. It was pitch dark. He put on the light and walked, heavy-hearted, up the uncarpeted stairs. He took out his keys, selected the one for the front door of the flat, and started to insert it before he noticed that the door wasn't shut properly. ' He frowned, and drew the key back.

The door was open an inch or two.

There was no light on inside, but he didn't push the door wider at first, just stood with his hands clenched, his eyes narrowing, depression gone. Barbara might have come here, she had a key; so had his father. Neither of them would have left the door open, that was unthinkable. He had switched on the light downstairs, and anyone hiding in here would have seen it, so there was no hope of taking anyone by surprise.

He remembered Richard's quip—before he went on more jaunts to the East End he would want a gun. Martin would have given a lot for a gun.

He heard no breath of sound.

He pushed the door open gently and stepped forward into the darkness. Gradually a faint light from behind him showed up the doors leading to the kitchen, the passage, and the living-room. He turned towards the living-room, and put out his hand; the door was open. He pushed it wider, groped for the light switch and pressed it down. As it came on, he stepped swiftly to one side.

Nothing happened.

He ventured forward, until he could see part of the room.

Jessica Rennie was tied to a chair facing the door; her eyes were wide open and shining with fear. A scarf was tied round her mouth, gagging her.

21 WARNING

MARTIN saw the desperate appeal in the girl's eyes, but didn't go to her. He raised a hand to try to reassure her, forced a smile, and peered round the side of the door. This room was empty. He didn't speak, but turned his back on her; he could imagine what she felt. He went into each of the rooms and made sure that the flat was completely empty, apart from Jessica. The small dressing-tables in his room and Richard's had been searched; drawers were open and oddments lay on the floor. He didn't worry about that. The lock of the front door was broken, and he took a kitchen-chair to it, jammed the chair beneath the handle, and so made sure that no one could come in and catch him by surprise. Then he took a glass of water into the living-room.

" It's all right," he said as he approached the girl. " I'll soon have you free."

He put the glass down on the table between the two arm-chairs, and took out his knife.

Jessica was tied to an upright chair, her wrists fastened together behind it; she was thrust forward, the position must be painful. He cut the cords gently, and didn't nick her flesh. She made a strange gasping sound behind the gag, and her body sagged. He cut the cords at her ankles, which were fastened to the legs of the chair, and then went behind her and untied the scarf. It was a cheap knitted woollen thing, tied tightly, and the knots were difficult to undo. He managed them; the scarf didn't fall free. He took it away carefully, and saw the deep ridges on either side of her mouth; there were more on her wrists and ankles, the job had been cruelly done. He lifted the girl and put her in his arm-chair, the larger of

163

the two, pushed a pouf into position and raised her legs on to it. Then he held the glass to her lips, and she tried to sip. Some of the water trickled down her chin and neck, but she swallowed some; even swallowing was an effort.

"Don't try to talk for a bit," Martin said. "Just take it easy."

He pulled up the upright chair, took her right hand, and began to massage it. She didn't whimper, although as the blood circulation started up, it must have been agony. He rubbed each wrist and her ankles. By then her cheeks were flushed to a beetroot red, and her eyes seemed to be made of glass.

"More water?"

She nodded. He gave her a little, then went to the kitchen and put on a kettle; a hot drink would do her more good than anything else. While it was boiling he went into each of the rooms. Evidence of a search was in the sitting-room, although a tidier job had been done there. Every drawer had been opened, and the contents were untidy; he couldn't see that anything had been taken away, although he would have to make a thorough search before he could be sure of that. He didn't ask himself yet what the burglars had been looking for.

He made the tea, poured out a cup and added plenty of sugar, and took it to Jessica. She now had enough strength in her right wrist to hold the cup. She drank noisily, and he stood watching her, questions flooding through his mind; he tried to stem them.

"Feel better?"

"Yes—ta."

"Try to tell me what happened," said Martin.

She began to talk, and had a nice economy of phrase. The story was disjointed, but he was able to piece it together easily. She had gone to the Strand Corner House for a meal, and then walked across to Leyden Lane. She had known no one would be there for a while, but hadn't wanted to go to the pictures, and had strolled up and down. It was cold, so she had stepped into the little porch outside the front door, to shelter from the wind. Then she had found that the door was open, she'd gone inside being sure that he wouldn't mind her taking shelter there. She'd walked up the stairs, not thinking of danger. As she had reached the boxed-in door to the flat it had opened and a man had leapt at her.

There had been two men; she knew neither of them.

They had tied her to the chair, and talked. They had not said a great deal, but the little went through Martin like a knife.

She was to tell him that if he wanted to see his brother or Kathleen Wilder again, he was to drop the case.

.   .   .   .   .

Martin turned to the telephone, mind bristling with alarm. As he stretched out his hand to call the Lasil Street Hotel, the bell rang sharply. Jessica was watching with eyes that were still frightened.

" Did they touch this? " he asked.

" No."

He lifted the telephone. " Hallo."

A man spoke quickly—a man whose voice he did not recognize and felt sure he had never heard before.

" Is that Martin Fane of Prince's? "

" Speaking."

" So you've arrived," said the man, still quickly. "Had a little talk with Jessie? "

Martin didn't answer; his grip on the telephone was painfully tight.

" Shock made you dumb? " asked the other, and the sneer in his voice reminded Martin of Rosa. " You'd better stay dumb as far as this job's concerned. She's told you to drop this case. Take her advice. Otherwise your brother will have a *very* bad time. Not to mention his girl friend. You ought to have seen her face when we took Richard in to say hello."

Martin said softly, " Don't hurt either of them."

" Oh, *no*? Remember what happened to Hicky Sharp?

Just keep it in mind, Fane. Shut up your office and go back to drawing for a living. Just because your father makes a pile writing about crime, that doesn't mean he has all the answers. Drop all of this business, and have the stuff ready to hand over. Otherwise you won't see either of them alive."

" What stuff——" began Martin.

The man rang off.

Martin replaced the receiver slowly, smiled mechanically at Jessica, and dialled the Lasil Street Hotel, speaking as he did so.

" It was one of the men who tied you up, telling me what you've already said. I'm just going to see if there's any truth in the story that my brother's disappeared."

" I—see."

A girl answered. " Lasil Street Hotel."

" Is Mr. Jonathan Fane there, please? "

" Hold on a moment, I'll call his room."

Martin held on, looking at Jessica without studying her. This had hit him hard; if it were true about Richard, it would be hell for his mother and father. Yet there was one thing that stood out; no one would go to these lengths to get him and Richard off the case unless they knew something that mattered; or at least, unless the people working for Clarke thought they knew. Stuff? What had the man meant?

His father came on the line.

" Hallo."

" This is Scoop."

" Oh," said Fane, and the very tone of his voice told Martin that the story was true. " We've had a nasty blow, old chap. You'd better come——"

" Richard? "

" How did you know? " Fane asked sharply.

Martin told him. Fane didn't respond at once; he was taking his time to think about the new development. Finally he said:

" Where are you? "

" At the flat."

" I'll come and see you and the girl," said Fane. " I've one or two other things to talk about, too. I'll be there in half an hour. I won't bring Barbara or your mother."

" Right-ho."

" Meanwhile, try to find out if they took anything that matters," said Fane.

" I'll do that," Martin promised.

He turned back to the girl and, without speaking, held out his hands. She took them and stood up. She was unsteady on her feet, but was able to hobble about after a few minutes. He let her hobble, supporting herself against chairs and tables, as he looked into the drawers which had been opened and searched. As far as he could judge, everything of value was still there. A locked drawer in a bureau had been forced, and fifty pounds in cash were untouched. So they hadn't come to steal, they had been looking for something specific.

What?

Any guess was as good as the next.

He examined the front door, and found a piece of mica sticking out at each side of the lock; the mica trick was an old one, but you had to be good to do it.

He went into the other rooms, but nothing appeared to be missing. In the living-room Jessica was sitting down again. She looked much better, and the high colour had gone. The ridges at her mouth and wrists were much fainter, too; she hadn't been tied up long enough for them to be really severe. He smiled as he dropped into a chair opposite her.

" Like some more tea? "

" No, ta."

" I hope you're feeling much better," said Martin. " This might cheer you up. I've seen your father, and I think there's a good chance that he won't have to appear in Court. Superintendent Kelby assured me of that. Provided he's told the truth, and provided you have too, there's nothing to worry about."

Jessica said flatly, " If the rozzers have got him they'll put him inside."

" I don't think so, Jessica. Any idea what the men who came here were looking for? "

Jessica looked at him with brooding eyes, was obviously thinking much more about her father than about the question, but after a while she answered:

" They said something about plates."

" Plates? " Martin echoed blankly.

" Yes—*plates.*"

Martin rubbed his chin, frowning—and the frown suddenly faded, excitement shone in his eyes. The girl was astonished by the change, and sat up a little. He gave a short, mirthless laugh, took out cigarettes, lit one, and put his lighter away.

" Plates! Now I see. Did they——"

The front-door bell rang. He turned abruptly and hurried to it, calling as he put a hand on the chair:

" Who's that? "

" All right, Scoop," said his father.

Martin pulled the chair away, and Fane came in and watched him as he put it back. Fane's eyes were clouded; the bleakness which the manager of the hotel had seen was gone, but the burden of a great anxiety was in them. It took away something of the youthfulness of his appearance, and Martin noticed that he limped much more than usual. Exceptional mental tension always made him do that.

He smiled cheerfully enough at Jessica.

" Hallo, young lady! I'm sorry about this."

" So'm I," said Jessica promptly.

" I don't blame you! "

" Jessica, go into the other rooms and tidy up for me, will you? " Martin asked. He led her to the door; she walked quite freely now, and did not argue. " Put everything back as neatly as you can, and we'll call you as soon as we're ready."

" Okay," said Jessica.

Martin went back to the big room, to find Fane standing with his back to the cupboard where they kept the liquor. Martin opened it, and took out whisky and a soda syphon. He didn't offer his father a drink; Fane had been a life-long teetotaller, and no stress or strain was likely to make him change that habit now.

Martin poured out a drink and said, "Jessica heard them talking about plates. Does that mean anything to you?"

"Of course." Fane didn't hesitate. "The plates from which these damned notes are printed. They weren't at Buckley Street or at Hicky Sharp's place, were they? No, I'm not psychic——" he smiled faintly. "I had a telephone call from one of these men, soon after I found that Richard was missing. He told me to tell you to hand the stuff over. I couldn't imagine what stuff—but the plates seem to be the answer. Why should they think you have them?"

"I can't imagine."

"It's possible that someone told them so," Fane said. He turned away from Martin, went across to one of the bookshelves and started to take books down, one after the other. "These have all been shifted, they're not in the usual order. Wonder they took the trouble to put them back. Er—Scoop." His tone was subdued, his manner tense. "We've always got along very well together. It's been one of the good things. I've always been sure that if you were in difficulty you'd tell me. I haven't been quite so certain of Richard, although I haven't had serious doubts. See what I'm driving at?"

Martin didn't answer.

Fane turned and faced him squarely.

"You do, of course. Now, let's have one thing very clear, old chap. You lead your own life in your own way. If I can help or advise, I'm happy to. But I don't want to interfere or thrust my way of living on you. I've certain standards and try to live up to them. Another good thing has been to see that you—and Richard, for

169

the most part—have similar standards. We talk the same language. Now, Scoop—if you know anything more than you've said, tell me. This idea of a business came very suddenly, or at least the practical development of it did. Also, Richard was already friendly with this Kathleen Wilder. Did you suspect there was anything wrong with her? Had you been working to find out what it was? Have you in fact got those plates, and are you holding them, in the hope that you'll be able to force the crooks into making a fatal slip? If you have, I won't argue about your keeping it from the police, for the time being. But I'd feel pretty bad about it if you didn't tell me, now, because it might be life or death to Richard. Be frank, won't you?"

HALF-WAY through his father's words Martin went to a chair, sat down, stretched his legs out, and looked up into the older man's face. He didn't smile, but sipped his whisky several times. When Fane had stopped, he didn't answer immediately. Fane poured himself out a tomato juice and drank half of it at one gulp; then he lit a cigarette—his fingers were already stained with nicotine. He made a solid, rather distinguished figure, and Martin was so obviously his son, although much leaner and an inch taller.

They could not hear Jessica moving about in the bedrooms.

Martin sat up and began to smile.

" That's a new notion as far as I'm concerned. I don't know anything you don't know. The whole thing began when Kathleen Wilder came here. Richard stayed in for her, and had laid it all on. The story stood up as far as I could see—they were puzzled by Clarke's behaviour. I think it possible that Richard was dubious about Rosa, but I doubt if he went deeply into it."

Fane said warmly, " Good! "

He finished his tomato juice, and went and sat down. There were slight curves at the corners of his mouth.

" Had you talked about the agency with Richard before? "

" No."

" It isn't very likely that you'd both nurse the same idea. It looks as if he was interested in Kathleen and thought up this way of introducing her to the family. How much do you know about his interest in the girl? "

" Exactly what I've told you. I'd no idea there was

anything serious afoot until she came here. Then I judged from Richard's manner that he wasn't having another light-hearted *affaire*; Kathleen mattered." Martin paused. " You'll like her."

" I'd like the chance to find out! Well, Scoop—we know where we stand. One thing is certain. Kelby thinks that you know more than you'll admit."

" Oh," said Martin.

Fane was reasonable.

" We can't be surprised. You came into this case quickly, and you've done some remarkable things. The way you rushed to Buckley Street and found them pulling up the floorboards was a bit too much for Kelby. He doubtless tells himself that you must have had some idea of what you'd find, or you wouldn't have gone there. Best assume that Kelby is highly suspicious. The Rennie contact is another thing that makes him dubious about you, of course. But he isn't sure. Before you arrived at the Yard to-night Niven had told me that the police are very worried about the forged notes. There are hundreds of thousands in circulation, on the black market overseas as well as at home, and they haven't been able to trace them until now. Clarke was one of the suspects because he was a paper-maker in a small way, led a rather peculiar life—seldom came home, travelled a great deal. Then they put a man into his factory and found that he had a little private mill, which he worked himself with one or two workmen. He was supposed to be making paper for special editions of books. Even before the murders were committed it was a big show. It's much bigger now. And if we're right—and I think we are—someone believes that you have those plates. It means you've a strong bargaining hand."

Martin nodded slowly.

" So I should go on letting them believe it," Fane said.

Martin didn't speak.

" Even if it makes Kelby even more suspicious," in- sisted Fane. " You won't always be able to do exactly what the police think you should. The next thing will be another call from the unknowns—they'll probably want to see you or a messenger, with the plates." He closed his eyes for a moment, and Martin watched intently. Discussing the situation had eased Fane's anxiety a little. " I wonder how long it would take to get a set of blocks made, Scoop."

Martin whistled.

Fane chuckled.

" The Prince would probably suggest that. Do you know a block-maker who——"

" I know exactly the man! He'll take some persuading, but he'll do it."

" The fewer people who are in the know, the better. Tell him it's a special advertising stunt, and you're in a hurry. Twenty-four hours should be enough. The plates needn't be really accurate, but something that will look all right at a quick glance. Then if you get a call, you can do some business. Get the thing set. We'll decide later whether to take Kelby into our confidence or not. I'm prepared to do anything to get Richard safely back."

Martin said, " Of course."

" So we still speak the same language."

Fane looked pleased.

" I fancy we shall for a long time."

" Yes. Now I must go and see your mother. She's taken it well, as you would imagine. Oh, there's another thing. I've already started Barbara on it, but you'll have to help. The Yard are doubtless working on it, but they haven't said so." He paused. " Know what I mean? "

" How long has Richard known Kathleen—and what can we find out about Kathleen's past? "

" That's right," said Fane.

" We mustn't forget that if it hadn't been for Kathleen, we should never have got on to this," Martin said.

" Who's forgetting? " asked Fane.

There was a lot to do, and too little time. Jessica was a problem on her own. Barbara might be able to find a bed for her—at her flat or else at a Girls' Hostel. Jessica wasn't likely to take kindly to a hotel, and a hotel was not likely to take very kindly to Jessica. Martin busied himself on the telephone, speaking to a friend of Richard's on *Charade*, learning what he could about Richard and Kathleen. They had been friendly for some weeks; the friend believed it was a serious case. Kathleen had no known troubles, was a promising young actress, no more.

Barbara arrived as soon as he had finished.

" Yes, I'll do something about Jessica," she said. " I know the matron at a hostel in Norfolk Street. If there's no room there I can find her a bed in one of the Y.W.C.A. hostels. I'll take her away at once, you needn't worry about it. The Maestro went into everything pretty closely with you, didn't he? "

" Yes."

" You try to fix those plates, and I'll be back," said Barbara.

Martin went to the telephone again, called a friend who worked for one of the big London block-makers; talked earnestly and long. Eventually he was promised a special job.

" I can't say I like the idea, but—O.K.," said the man.

" Thanks," said Martin warmly.

This might lead to complications which his father hadn't foreseen. The Maestro looked at everything from the angle of a book, his characters could twist events to suit themselves; Martin couldn't. Now that the arrangements were made he began to doubt their wisdom. The fact that Richard was missing nagged at him constantly. He thought less about Kathleen, but a lot about Rosa. Another factor came into his mind; no one else had yet mentioned it, but he did not doubt that Kelby had considered it. Why had Kathleen been kidnapped?

It hadn't been simply to get her out of the flat.

It was possible that the kidnappers, believing that the

Fane brothers had the plates, hoped to exert pressure on them by taking Kathleen away. Why, then, had they taken Richard? He would be the most likely victim of pressure about Kathleen.

Barbara wasn't back. Martin doubted if he could do much more to-night; it was nearly eleven. The Licker Club would still be open, but they wouldn't know much about Richard and Kathleen there. Kathleen was the real problem, and the police had doubtless been working on her at pressure for some hours. The odds against private individuals getting results, where the police had failed, seemed absurdly long. Gloom descended again.

The telephone bell rang. He hoped it was Barbara.

" Hallo? "

" Is that Mr. Martin or Mr. Richard Fane? "

" Martin Fane speaking."

The girl at the other end obviously knew nothing of the latest developments.

" Hold on, please, I have a personal call for you from Lichen Abbas, near Dorchester."

Martin said, " I'll hold on."

Lichen Abbas was the village where his parents lived; deep in rural Dorset, near the county town of Dorchester. Martin held on for what seemed a long time, fighting against the threat of a new anxiety. Then the operator spoke briskly:

" You're through."

" Thank yo', ma'am." A deep, rich voice came on the line. " Massa Martin, is dat yo'? "

Martin exclaimed, " Sampson! "

" Yassah, dis is Sampson," said the man at the other end. " Massa Martin, I sho' is a worried man. I just can't tell yo' how worried I is. I called you because I can't get at his hotel, but I positively must speak to one ob yo'." That deep but worried voice was of a Jamaican negro, who had served Jonathan Fane for years—since he had visited the West Indies on a world tour. Sampson was in charge at Nairn Lodge, loyal and thoroughly reliable—and now unhappy. The threat of the new anxiety drew darker.

" Let's have it," Martin said.

" Massa Martin, yo' won't neber believe what a shock I had, nossah. Neber in all yo' life. And if I hadn't took it into dis old head of mine to go wash-down the car, sah, and if I hadn't fo'got to lock up de garage, and so gone out ob my warm bed to go an' lock it up, sah, I guess I would neber hab found it."

" Found what, Sampson? " Martin knew that patience was needed; knew also that Sampson would not ramble on like this unless he had really received a nasty jolt.

" Massa Martin, yo' neber would believe it. Moment I set my eyes on dat turrible sight, I began to shiber, an' I guess my hand is now shaking so much I can hardly hold de telephone. It put me right in mind ob dat time when dere was de body in dat car ob yours."

Martin said softly, " Go on, Sampson."

There was a body in the garage; it surely couldn't be Richard's. Sampson wouldn't talk like this if it were Richard's. But Sampson's voice betrayed his jitters, and Sampson hardly knew how to say what he had to say, so—it *could* be Richard.

Or Kathleen.

" I done make sure de man is dead, Massa Martin, 'fore I called you. He's dead all right. His head's something turrible to look at."

Martin said slowly, " Do you know him, Sampson? "

" No, sah ! "

" All right." A wave of relief came. " Who have you told? "

" I ain't told no one, sah," said Sampson indignantly. " The minute I see dat body, I locked up de garage and come to de telephone. You consider I ought to telephone de police? "

" No," said Martin. " I'll do that. I'll come right down."

" Yo' sho' hab made me feel better, Massa Martin. Can yo' tell Massa Jon what's happened, without telling de missus? It sho' would be a mighty big shock fo' her."

" Yes, I'll tell my father. You wait up, and don't touch anything. Watch the garage, but don't let yourself be seen. Try and remember if you've seen any strangers——"

" Ain't seen no stranger to-day, that's certain sho'. They must hab come after dark, and I was so careless I left de do' unlocked. I'm sorry about dat, Massa Martin."

Sampson sounded as if he were in the depth of misery.

" You've done fine. I'll be down as soon as I can. It'll be about three o'clock, I expect."

" I'll be waitin', sah! Good-bye right now."

" Good-bye, old chap."

Martin put the receiver down and stared at it; pictured the negro's dark, shining face, his grey hair, his easy smile. He had been brought up with Sampson; knew the man well, and loved him. Sampson was frightened; and small wonder. But there would surely be no more danger to-night. It wouldn't help to tell the police——

He stopped thinking, and called his father.

Ten minutes later he was on his way to Dorset.

The roads were empty. He picked up some petrol at a garage on the outskirts of the West End; that would see him to Nairn Lodge. He drove faster than even Richard would drive; the Buick hurtled through the cold, dark night, casting great beams of light. In two and a quarter hours—the journey by day took four hours— he passed through the little village near the house, and three minutes afterwards swung the car into the drive. Now the headlights shone on the wooded banks on either side of the drive; soon, on the square Georgian outlines of the building itself. The white-painted shutters showed up; Sampson had closed them all.

Branches of wistaria grew over the front porch and round some of the shutters; there was a charm about the house, even in these small hours. The garage was at

M   177

one side, out of sight from the drive itself. As Martin slowed down outside the front door it opened. Sampson, dressed in a big coat and wearing a hat, came on to the porch to welcome him. The light was on behind him.

Martin jumped out.

"Massa Martin, am I glad to see yo'!" Sampson gripped Martin's arm with both his hands. "There ain't been another sound, no sir, no one's come. The body's still jus' where I found it."

"All right, I'll go," said Martin. "You needn't come."

"I better come."

Sampson took a large flash-light out of his pocket and walked by Martin's side towards the garage. One door was partly open, the other was closed. He put the torch into Martin's hand as they reached the door.

Martin opened the door wider.

Two cars were in the garage, and there was room for a third. The body lay in a corner on its side. Sampson didn't come right into the garage, but Martin could hear his teeth chattering.

"Put on the light," Martin said.

"Sho'—sho' thing, sah."

The powerful light from the ceiling blazed down, on to the battered head and the pale, pudgy face. The side of the head had been blown in, and an old Service type revolver lay near a lifeless hand. Martin didn't know the face, but the name which sprang to his mind was Clarke. The build and description certainly tallied.

He went nearer, and slid his hand into the inside coat pocket, drew out a wallet, and found a letter inside, addressed to Clarke.

23

MARTIN sat in his father's study, at the telephone. Sampson stood by the door. This was a room he seldom visited unless Fane were here; he was used to seeing the burly, shirt-sleeved figure in front of the typewriter, which was now covered with its black hood; like a shroud.

"Yes, I'm pretty sure it's Clarke," Martin said. "I found his name on letters in his pocket. I should say he killed himself—that's what it looks like, anyhow."

"Looks like is about right." Jonathan Fane sounded very near, although he was still at the Lasil Street Hotel. "We can be pretty sure this is a diversion. Whoever has done this wanted you off the case. He tried by high-pressuring you, and seems to think that won't work, so he's tried a new game. If the police are busy with you, you won't have much time to spare hunting round on your own."

Martin rubbed one eye, which was already red-rimmed, but made no comment.

"Yet it seems to cut across the effort to get those plates from you," Fane went on. "Unless——" He broke off. Martin knew that he wrote his books much as he was talking now; let words run on, then seized upon ideas which flowed almost as smoothly as the words. "Unless they think you'll keep this from the police. Clarke comes down to Nairn Lodge, your home, and—kills himself. That's what it *looks* like. Now if you or I or any of us had a guilty conscience, what should we do? Withhold the information from the police, shouldn't we?"

Martin grunted.

"If we did that, the killer would be after us. Yes,"

179

went on Fane, and sounded excited, carried away by this new notion. " If the dead man is Clarke, then someone else is involved—someone we don't know. This someone thinks that you and Richard know a lot more than you do. Following me? "

" Yes."

" In fact, the someone already makes it clear he thinks a Fane has those plates. In other words, thinks a Fane was working *with* Clarke."

" Yes," conceded Martin.

Fane didn't speak for several seconds. Sampson, looking more miserable than ever, shifted his feet. His coat was still buttoned tightly, and his thick underlip drooped and was thrust forward. Martin didn't move, except to rub his eye, which was tickling.

" The question is, shall we tell the police or not? " Fane spoke briskly. " If we tell them, they'll send the Dorchester police to the Lodge, and Kelby might even go down himself. I can't imagine them sitting on the discovery and pretending to know nothing about it. On the whole I think it's a case of taking a chance. Lock the garage up and say nothing. Only Sampson knows the truth." Fane paused. " What do you think? "

Martin said slowly, " Well, this chap seems to take it for granted that we're involved. Why should he? It's true that we've made ourselves sitting birds. You made it clear that some of the things I've done have suggested to Kelby that I know plenty. Richard's chase after Hicky Sharp did more. Now if the police find a body in the garage they'll feel pretty sure that we're involved. Someone has cashed in on the position we helped to create and wants to switch the attention of the police to us. Why? "

" Don't make it too involved," Fane cautioned. " When it's all over we'll find there's a fairly simple explanation. We're speculating too much. I still think the wise thing to do would be to say nothing to the police. Remember no one's to know when we find the body in the garage. We can make the discovery whenever we like. Sampson wouldn't have gone there at all if he hadn't forgotten to lock it. We might have come back on Monday or Tuesday and found it then. The police can't prove we've held anything back. Our hand is fairly strong. Sit on it, Martin. Unless——"

He paused.

" Yes? "

" Unless you feel strongly that the police ought to be told."

Martin said in a harsh voice, " I don't care a damn what risks I run, provided we get Richard out of this mess. If we set the police against us as an agency it can't be helped. Richard's the only consideration."

" Sit back and say nothing," advised Fane. " Have a few hours' sleep, and get here as early as you can in the morning. I shall *not* tell your mother yet. It might be advisable to tell Barbara."

" I shall tell her."

" By the way, she's got Jessica into a Y.W.C.A. No need to worry about the girl." It was characteristic of Fane to remember a small thing at that juncture. " Oh— get the garage keys from Sampson. Tell him to say nothing, whatever happens or whoever questions him, and to telephone here if he is questioned. Don't worry about his jitters, he'll get over them. If you tell him Richard's life is at stake, he'll convince Kelby and Niven rolled up in one that he's never been inside that garage since we left. All clear? "

" Yes. Thanks."

" Fine! " said Fane. " Make sure you get those few hours' sleep. You'll need them."

.   .   .   .   .

Sampson took the instructions with a harassed air, but swore secrecy. No one else knew Martin had arrived. He was in bed at four o'clock and up again just after seven. He had learned the trick of doing without long stretches of sleep at a time; unlike his father. He was on the road by half-past seven, and in London a little before eleven. He telephoned the Lasil Street Hotel from a call-box in Roehampton; every one of the family was out. He telephoned the office; his mother answered him.

"Why, hallo!" Martin tried to sound bright.

"Oh, Scoop! Have you any news?"

"Afraid not," said Martin. "I was hoping you would have."

"Nothing at all," said Evelyn Fane miserably. "Your father told me you had been working all night on the case. Don't overdo it, darling. It won't help if you're tired out, and you'll need all your wits about you."

"I'll be all right. Seen Barbara?"

"Yes, she's doing the best she can to find out more about this Kathleen girl. Your father's been at Scotland Yard for the past hour. *I'm* here dealing with the callers, there have been dozens. You'll have to get some help in the office, and you *must* get a carpet. It's impossible."

Martin was speechless.

"Jessica——" he said at last.

"Barbara's fitting her out with some serviceable clothes, and she's coming here this morning. Oh—Rennie's been released."

"Good."

"I'm not so sure it is good," said Evelyn. "The girl seems to have her head screwed on properly, though. I would never have believed that I should find myself acting as a receptionist and getting ready to tell *her* what to do. I—oh, damn it, there's that beastly buzzer again. Scoop——"

"Yes, mother?"

"Be very careful," Evelyn said.

Martin rang off, and smiled faintly as he went to the car. He couldn't get that "you must have a carpet" out of his mind—and the really significant fact that his mother had withdrawn her opposition and was now fully behind them; it could mean nothing else. He had expected the danger to Richard to push her the other way; she was quite unpredictable—except to his father.

He stood by the side of the Buick, trying to decide what to do. He could go to the office and wait for Barbara; waiting didn't appeal to him. He could go to Scotland Yard; obviously it would be wiser to wait and find out what his father had been doing there. He could dig into Kathleen's past; but that might be doubling the work which Barbara was already doing. He felt lonely and impotent.

A man approached him from a corner, walking briskly, with an unlit cigarette at his lips. He stopped.

" Got a light, mister? "

Martin took out his lighter.

The man puffed out smoke.

" Thanks," he said, and drew back. " Want to see your brother again? "

.   .   .   .   .

The question came out of the blue. The man was just an ordinary little nondescript individual, in the thirties. He grinned as he put the question. He wasn't menacing in any way; didn't look as if he could be menacing.

Martin said, " What's that?."

" You heard. I've been following you from Kingston By-pass, you want to keep your eyes open wider. Got those plates yet? "

" No," Martin said stonily.

" That's a lie. We know you've got them. We know you've been home and seen Clarke, too. Like me to nip in there and telephone your pal Kelby? Perhaps he wouldn't be so pally if he knew you'd got Clarke's body at your father's country house, would he? " The man grinned again. His tone was casual, they might have been talking about the weather. People passed, on foot, on cycles, and in cars; and no one looked at them twice. " Time you made up your mind, mister, we want those plates."

" What plates? "

The man leaned nearer, and drew deeply at his cigarette.

" Chum, you're not so dumb as all that. Don't come it. You've got the plates. When we've got them you can have your precious brother back, and his girl. Until then——" The man shrugged, and drew back. " See what I mean? "

Martin looked at him steadily and then said :

" Yes. Of course, I could break your neck."

" Not a chance." There was no hint of fear in the pale-blue eyes. " Not a chance in a thousand, Mister Fane. We've got you where we want you. You go along to your office, Fane, and we'll call you with instructions."

" What's the matter with giving them to me now? "

" They'll come when we're ready," the man said.

He took his cigarette from his lips, tossed it into the road, put a hand to his forehead in a mock salute, and turned away. He was two yards off when Martin moved, and he didn't hear Martin coming. Martin gripped his arm behind him in a hammer-lock and forced him round towards the Buick. He didn't speak as he opened the door. No one was passing, except two motorists who noticed nothing. The man turned a scared face, and was more scared when he saw Martin's expression.

" Get in."

" Listen——"

" Get in! "

The man climbed into the seat next to the wheel. Martin let him go, and dipped his hand into the man's right pocket ; his fingers closed over a gun. He transferred it to his own pocket, and said :

" Rather than let you go, I'll shoot you. Don't forget it. Look up there."

He glanced upwards, and the man did the same. Martin jabbed an upper-cut to his chin, as it stuck out ; the man gasped and collapsed. Martin hurried to the other side of the car. No one had noticed the incident, and the man was right out. Martin stepped on the accelerator, but hadn't made up his mind where to go. The flat seemed the best bet. He drove there, with the gun in his right-hand pocket. The man came round, but was dazed and helpless. Martin swung into Leyden Lane, turned into the waste plot, jammed on the brakes, and said:

" Out you get. Don't try to run."

He pushed the man towards the door. He meant it when he said that he would shoot; nothing would make him let this man escape. He could see customers in the grocery shop, people hurrying towards it, a car turning the corner. His prisoner walked ahead of him like a dazed rabbit.

The car drew level. There was a sharp report, like the backfire of an engine. The prisoner staggered, half-turned, and then fell on his face.

The car roared towards the end of the street.

THE prisoner was dead; a bullet had caught him behind the ear. A crowd had already gathered, silenced by the suddenness and the obvious horror. The noise of the car had merged into the sounds of London traffic. Martin stared at the dead man and then at a little woman at the front of the crowd, and tried to think straight. He hadn't time to consult his father; there was no way of keeping this from the police. Directly Kelby knew where it had happened he would come racing over.

A policeman, with two men by his side, was already hurrying towards the spot—three yards from Martin's front door.

Martin turned, pushed his way through the crowd, knew there wasn't a chance to get the Buick out, and strode along the narrow lane. He had gone twenty yards before anyone realized what he was doing, and several people called out. A youth began to run. Martin didn't. He swung round the corner, crossed the road, and took another turning; he was soon in the Strand. He didn't know whether he had been followed all the way, and didn't care. He reached the office block, and ran for the first time—up the stairs. He flung open the outer door. His mother was sitting at a desk, reading a magazine; it looked like *Vogue*. Martin pushed up the flap of the counter, stepped through, caught his toe against a floorboard which stuck up a fraction of an inch, and pitched forward; only a table saved him from falling.

His mother jumped up.

" One of you *will* break your neck unless you have this floor covered."

Martin steadied himself by the table.

" Yes, we'll have to see about it. Dad in? "

" No. Scoop, what's happened? " Evelyn needed no telling that there was more trouble. " Don't stand there glaring at me, *what's happened*? "

" I took a prisoner, and he was shot."

His mother drew in a sharp breath.

" I must see Dad before I talk to the police," said Martin. " He——"

" Must you? " asked his mother quietly. " I wonder, Martin."

She only called him Martin if she were in deadly earnest; never affectionately, never emotionally. He glanced round at the door, and she seemed to guess that he thought that he might have been followed, so she hurried across and pushed the bolt home. A shadow appeared at the door, a man pushed it—and then the buzzer sounded.

" Let's go in here," said Evelyn Fane, and led the way into Martin's own office. " Martin, I don't know what it is, but I do know your father is keeping something from me. I suspect that you know what it is. He only does things like that to save my feelings, but he ought to know better by now, it only makes me feel worse."

The buzzer went again, and the sound lasted much longer.

" So tell me what it is," said Evelyn. " Martin, I love your father desperately, but he does get the wildest ideas. How can he help it? He lives in a world of his own making, but he can't make the real world like that. He can't deal with Scotland Yard as his characters would— you'd all be in prison within a week! I have a feeling that he's advising you about this, and you've taken some desperate chance that might lead to serious trouble. If that's so—what *is* it? "

There was a thud at the door, and then a man called out in a deep voice:

" I don't want to *make* trouble, Mr. Fane."

187

" If that isn't a policeman, I've never heard one," Evelyn said.

Martin found himself smiling in spite of himself.

" That's a policeman," he agreed. " I'd better go and let him in."

He knew that by the evasion he had confirmed his mother's suspicions, and the appealing look in her eyes was hurtful. As he reached the counter he forgot that; for his father's voice sounded clearly.

" Hallo, what's all this? "

" I want to see your son, Mr. Fane. I know he's inside." The voice was vaguely familiar, and had an authoritative ring. " I don't know what he's up to, but I don't like his attitude."

" Martin? He's a most reasonable chap," said Fane. " Have you been coming the old soldier with him, Chief Inspector? "

" I have not. Will you tell him to open the door? "

" Martin——" began Fane.

Martin opened the door, nodded to his father, and looked into the set face of Chief Inspector Oakes— Kelby's chief *aide*. Oakes was a big, barrel-like man with a weather-beaten face and piercing grey eyes. He had a shock of grey hair which wouldn't lie flat.

Fane stepped in. Two or three people stood on the landing, looking in curiously. Oakes followed Fane and closed the door.

" Mr. Fane, I understand that you were going into your flat with a man, who was shot from a passing car, and that instead of waiting to give what information you could to the police you ran away. Is that true? "

" Ran is an exaggeration," said Martin calmly. " I came away."

" Why? "

" I wanted time to think."

" I don't believe you," Oakes said flatly. " You wanted time to do something. What was it? What are you hiding from us? Do you think murder is a matter for trifling? "

Martin said, " I wanted time to think. The man had accosted me in the street, threatened me, said that he knew where my brother was. I forced him to get into my car and was going to question him. He was obviously followed and shot."

" I see," said Oakes coldly. " I take it——"

He broke off, for the outer door was thrust open, and Kelby came in; a glowering Kelby. His eyes glittered and his hands were clenched; Martin hadn't seen him angry before. He moved more softly than usual, approached Martin, then put his head back, and said:

" I warned you, didn't I? I warned you not to play the fool. Now you've let a man die. If you——"

" Nonsense! "

" So it's nonsense, is it? " breathed Kelby. " I see. It's nonsense when you take a man to your flat for questioning instead of bringing him to Scotland Yard? It's nonsense when we say that by doing that you were responsible to the Yard. We'll see what's nonsense, Mr. Fane. Your father's romantic ideas might work in books, but they won't work in real life."

As he echoed Evelyn's words, she moved forward; it was the first time she had shown herself since the police had arrived. Fane shot her a warning glance; but she was in no mood to accept his warning.

" Who on earth do you think you are? " she flared.

Kelby glowered.

" Mrs. Fane——"

" Don't you Mrs. Fane me! Who do you think you are, and what do you think you're doing? My husband is worth you, *that* man, and the rest of the officers at Scotland Yard put together. He has more ideas in one morning on the typewriter than you have in a year." Her voice grew shrill. " Don't you come into *our* offices talking as if you owned them. You don't. You may have a reputation at Scotland Yard, but it hasn't reached here. Why, if you——"

189

" Evelyn, my dear——" Fane began.

" You be quiet! It's time this *ox* had a piece of my mind. You're too soft with policemen. They want telling what the public thinks of them. Why, I've had fifteen people come in this morning, offering us work, and all of them have complained that the police won't listen to what they have to say. *All* of them——"

" Be quiet! " roared Kelby.

" Don't you shout at me! "

Oakes was looking red and embarrassed, Kelby tried to control himself, and was obviously having a difficult job, Fane was now mildly amused; Martin stood by, stony-faced, and thinking hard. He caught his father's eye, and they moved aside.

" Now Mrs. Fane, I didn't mean to be offensive," Kelby began, in a placatory effort which obviously cost him dear. " If you would only realize——"

" I am *not* a fool," said Evelyn Fane with great deliberation. " The mistake that you people at Scotland Yard seem to make . . ."

She went on at some length. Kelby fumed, Oakes turned redder—and watched Martin and Fane, who were talking in whispers which were drowned by Evelyn's acid voice. Oakes edged towards the two men, but Evelyn moved, as if by accident, and prevented him from getting near.

" This all true? " whispered Fane.

" Yes. Chap knew about Clarke."

" Told Oakes or anyone? "

" No. I think we should."

" Why? "

" Only get into a worse mess if we keep it back."

" Don't you believe it." Fane's whisper was emphatic. " It's still a card up our sleeve. They've no way of telling when we found it. Don't forget that. We need a card. These other people are desperate, there's no question about that. Never mind what Kelby says now. We've got to lead the other side into making a mistake—

and we can only do it by making them think we're scared of the police. Hold your horses."

". . . and now I hope you're in no doubt as to my opinion of the police," Evelyn said icily.

Kelby breathed, " No, none. And I hope you're in no doubt as to my opinion of your son. Mr. Martin Fane! " His voice was a bellow. " I must ask you to come with me to Scotland Yard, Mr. Fane."

Evelyn opened her mouth as if to protest again. Fane stepped swiftly to her side, gripped her arm, and quietened her. Martin turned slowly, put his head on one side— and actually smiled. It might have been calculated to put the finishing touch to Kelby's rage; whether calculated or not, it succeeded. His eyes flamed, and he said:

" You'll laugh on the other side of your face when we've finished with you."

" Why——" began Evelyn explosively.

" Hush! " breathed Fane. " Leave this to Martin."

Martin's smile grew broader.

" I see. How are you going to do it, Mr. Kelby? "

" I'm going to take you to Scotland Yard. If you won't come without it, I'll charge you——"

" With what? "

" Withholding information——"

" That's no offence."

" Then I'll charge you with endeavouring to arrange the manufacture of photographic blocks of treasury notes for the purpose of forging treasury notes, and——"

" Oh, be yourself," snapped Martin; and Evelyn gasped again, but at last began to smile. She squeezed Fane's hand. " That's not the case, and you know it. It's true I asked a man to make a set of plates, but I needed them to help find Clarke. Find a charge that will stick."

" Will you, or will you not come with me? "

" Not until I know why you want me."

" To explain why you took this man to your flat instead

191

of bringing him to Scotland Yard. To explain how you happened to discover where the forged notes were. To explain why you're so friendly towards Rennie, an ex-convict with half a dozen convictions. To explain why you went to Dorset last night in such a hurry."

Kelby broke off, and for the first time since he had arrived a gleam of triumph appeared in his eyes; or what he obviously thought to be triumph. It didn't take Martin's smile away, although the last statement had given him a jolt. He had guessed already that he had been watched at the flat—probably both Leyden Lane and the office were being watched by the police all the time. Kelby suspected that he knew more than he did, and Kelby thought that he had the upper hand.

" Well? " demanded Kelby.

" No need to waste my time at the Yard. Half of that I've already told you. As for the rest—I went to Dorset to meet a man who told me that he'd talk about my brother there, but nowhere else. He didn't turn up— at least, I didn't see him." Martin lit a cigarette as he slid out of that one. " Have you found Miss Wilder or my brother yet? "

" No, and I never shall, if——"

" That's just about right," said Martin acidly. " You never will, if we leave it to you, Get this quite clear, Superintendent. My brother has been kidnapped, and you haven't been able to do a thing about it. You and all the Yard put together can't stop me from looking for him. If you try to prevent me by arresting me on some footling charge you know won't stick, it'll be plastered all over the newspapers to-night and to-morrow morning. *I'm* ready to co-operate. All you do is talk, and I'm tired of talking. I want action."

Kelby looked at him steadily throughout all this; and when he finished, turned abruptly on his heel. Only Oakes, following quickly, saved the door from slamming. Evelyn gave a little hysterical laugh, rushed to Martin and squeezed his arm. Fane smoothed down his hair and looked almost smugly satisfied.

" Scoop, I didn't think you had it in you," said Evelyn. " *That* will teach Kelby to talk to you as if you were one of his lackeys! " She gave the little laugh again, and tightened her grip on his hand. " But now tell me why you *did* go to Nairn Lodge."

25

AFTER Martin had told her, his mother walked slowly to a chair, dropped into it, looked first at Martin and then at her husband, and slowly shook her head, as if she despaired of ever understanding them. Fane winked at Martin.

" It's no use winking," Evelyn said. " Of all the idiots, you two are—but I can't blame Martin. You're the one responsible, Jon. What on earth will happen if Kelby discovers it? "

" Martin's told you, we won't go into that again now," said Fane briskly. " These other people are sure that we're hiding the body because we're involved. Let them go on thinking so. We'll hear from them——"

" You'll hear from *me* before this is over," said Evelyn. Her eyes were clouded. " Jon, do you really think this is the most likely way to help Richard? "

" Of course. There have been four murders. Obviously the devils might kill Richard. We have to play our hand to prevent that."

After a tense pause Evelyn said in a husky voice:

" We can't be sure he isn't dead, can we? "

" Now don't get that into your head." Fane was brisk. " While we have something they want, Richard will be all right. The plates and forged notes we haven't got are our bargaining weapons. We'll soon hear from the beggars. Scoop, keep up your attitude with Kelby if necessary. I've been talking to Niven this morning. I know him fairly well. Kelby realizes that, and won't want to upset a friend of his—he'll need to have a very strong hand before he can put you on a charge. I don't think you need worry about it."

194

His manner was deliberately tuned to keep Evelyn steady; he had even annoyed her in order to take her mind off the real burden of fear.

The door opened as he spoke, and Barbara came in. He smiled; even Evelyn smiled, as if she were forcing back her fears. Barbara, so tall and graceful, brought a breath of relief into the room, cleared it of the tension that had been here since Martin had returned.

She went straight to Evelyn.

" Sorry I've left you so long, Mother. I had quite a job getting Jessica fitted out. I've decided that it would be silly to bring her to the office until this is all over, so she's at my flat helping my daily woman. She's getting on quite nicely."

" Good," said Evelyn without much enthusiasm.

Barbara brushed her hair back absently.

" I've found out a little more about Kathleen, but I don't know that it helps much. She comes from a good middle-class family. There's never been any whisper against her good name; she's in earnest about acting, prefers the stage to the screen. Richard has known her casually for six months or so, and they've seen a lot of each other for the past few weeks. One or two of her friends say that they've had the impression that Kathleen was worried about something recently, but it's all rather vague. There are one or two rumours that she's quarrelled with Rosa Harding, but nothing definite."

" Now *that's* a woman I distrust," said Evelyn, as if she were divulging information no one suspected.

" Barbara doesn't think so much of her," Martin said.

" She's just a sexy menace," said Barbara. " What's been happening here? "

They told her; and as she listened, sitting with her ankles crossed and blowing occasionally at a wisp of hair, the buzzer sounded. There had been few callers in the last hour, Evelyn had dealt with the rush. This caller was a small boy, with a belt round his waist and a small leather pouch fastened to it.

" Mr. Martin Fane? " he piped.

" Yes."

Martin went across.

" Special delivery, Mr. Fane." With great care the lad opened the pouch, took out an envelope and a small book, handed them both to Martin with a flourish, and added, " Sign please."

Martin signed; and gave the lad sixpence.

" Coo, ta," he breathed, and went off, beaming.

Martin opened the letter. The others watched him intently, but he didn't hurry. His mother started to speak, but bit on the words. He took out the single fold of paper; the letter was written in block capitals which it would be impossible to identify. There wasn't much of it.

He read it silently at first, and then aloud:

" It's come. Listen: ' You will meet my messenge at Piccadilly Tube Station, by the Regent Street subway, at five o'clock this afternoon. Have everything with you. If you fail, you won't see either of them again. Don't tell the police. Remember what happened to S and to C.' "

.   .   .   .   .

" Five o'clock," said Evelyn in a strangled voice. " It's not one yet. We can't wait as long as that."

" It'll soon pass," Fane said.

Evelyn turned on him; he had meant her to. She was still talking when the door opened, without a preliminary ring at the buzzer, and Rennie came in.

.   .   .   .   .

Rennie had shaved and washed, and wore a clean shirt and clean muffler. His old, patched coat and his dirty cap were the same, and the shave wasn't a clean one, but he looked much more wholesome. His rather small eyes held a hint of a smile, as he stood and looked at the Fanes and Barbara, his head on one side, in an attitude of almost mocking amusement.

196

He touched the peak of his cap.

" Anyone at 'ome? "

Martin said, " Yes.   Come in, Rennie."

" Okay."   Rennie lifted the flap in the counter and marched in.   " Where's my Jess? "

" At my flat—perfectly all right," said Barbara.

" Better make sure she stays that way," said Rennie. He relaxed, and the mockery vanished from his eyes.   " I wouldn't have believed it, Guv'nor, but they said they accepted my story.   In a proper daze, I was, when I walked out of Cannon Row.   You must be able to work miracles.   Any trouble? "

He seemed to understand there was.

" Plenty."

Martin told him about Richard.

" That's bad," said Rennie.   " That's *very* bad, guv'nor.   I'm sorry abaht it."

" Rennie."   Fane spoke quietly.   " How did you know that Richard was at Ribley Court yesterday? "

" Saw 'im," said Rennie.   " Keepin' an eye on *H*icky Sharp, I was."   The grin touched his lips and eyes. " *H*icky meant money to me.   I can use plenty!   Been very int'rested in 'is pals, too."

Martin said softly, " Did you see anyone else at Ribley Court? "

" Oh, sure.   Couple of men.   Never seen 'em afore. Went off on a bike that was parked rahnd the back— there's a wooden fence wiv a n'ole in it, the rozzers were so quick they didn't find aht abaht it until arterwards."

" Recognize them? " Martin demanded.

" Can't say I did," said Rennie.   " But I did anovver job for you, guv'nor.   I was wiv a pal—Sammy Day. Quite a pal o' the police, Sammy is, just mention 'is name to Kelby and you'll see purple smoke."   The grin had never been broader.   " Never 'ad no proper chance to speak to Sammy, the rozzers pinched me, but I've just 'ad a word from 'im.   Guess what Sammy did? "

" How much do you want? " Fane demanded abruptly.

Rennie, who had been looking at Martin while he talked, shifted his gaze and bent upon Fane such a look of contempt that Fane was taken aback. A different man showed in Rennie then; a shadow of the man he had once been, and of the man he might become again.

"You're 'is old man, I s'pose. Well, *'e's* a gentleman. I don't charge for services rendered when I've 'ad a square deal. See?" He turned his back on Fane. "Sammy follered those guys. 'E 'ad a bike 'andy. Went to an 'ouse in Wimbledon, funny-looking place, looks as if the top 'arf's been taken off, Sammy says. Called The Beams—Common Rise. Any 'elp to you?"

   •   •   •   •   •

"So it's Rosa," said Martin in a strangled voice. "That *woman*."

"Or the man Henderson," Fane said.

"What are we going to do?" asked Barbara.

Evelyn snapped, "Tell the police, of course. I've no love for Kelby, but once he knows this he's bound to go to that house."

"That's right," said Fane. "And Henderson and Rosa will be watching, and the moment the police arrive, Richard will be on the spot. They've killed four times; another murder won't worry them."

Evelyn caught her breath.

"Sunnink in you writer blokes arter all," said Rennie, as if surprised. "The way this job's bin done, they'll cut your throat first an' arst your name arterwards. I never did like *H*icky Sharp or the company 'e kept."

"What are we going to *do*?" cried Evelyn.

Martin said, "We'll see. Thanks, Rennie, you've been a great help. If you'd like to see Jessica, the address is——"

"No, ta. She wouldn't like it if she's in a posh place and I turned up. I'll go and 'ave one."

He glared at Fane, as if daring him to put his hand in his pocket, and went out with a swagger. The door

198

closed loudly behind him. Downstairs the police were watching; Kelby probably already knew that Rennie had been here.

"What *are* we going to do?" Evelyn stood up. "Can't anybody say something?"

"It's difficult——" began Fane.

"It isn't," said Martin quietly—but he made them all swing round towards him. "Dad, you'll keep the appointment at Piccadilly. You'll tell the police about it, or else I will. The obvious thing is for them to be watching and follow the man. You'll take the plates, which should be ready by now."

Fane nodded slowly.

"While you're doing that I'll go to Wimbledon," said Martin. "It's dark at five, they won't see me until I get to the house. It's possible that I'll be followed, but I'll shake the follower off somehow. When Henderson or Rosa—they must be in it together, surely—are expecting to hear from their man——"

He paused. Fane opened his mouth, and Evelyn kicked him on the ankle. He winced—but smiled and nodded; let Martin have his head.

"I'd better get there about half-past five, just a little earlier. The messenger will almost certainly telephone a report. If he's collected the things, Rosa and Henderson will think they're sitting pretty. They won't expect me. At a quarter—no, at half-past five—Barbara will telephone the Yard. She'll tell Kelby that she's just heard from me, and I'm at The Beams. That should give me ten minutes or so to deal with the situation there before the police arrive. I shall probably need some help by then."

Evelyn closed her eyes.

"That about meets the case, I think," Fane said. "Didn't you say you took a gun off that man who was shot?"

Martin just touched his pocket.

.   .   .   .   .

Wilfred Henderson sat back in an easy-chair in the huge

drawing-room at The Beams, and smiled at his new wife. They had been married that morning by special licence. The room was beautifully furnished, practically every piece in it was antique. There were heavy wine-red velvet curtains, a wine-red carpet, and, in one corner, a huge grand piano. It was quiet, but a radio, tuned low, was switched on. Henderson, ankles crossed, plump face smiling gently at his wife, as if he could think of nothing else, drank his tea.

"And to-morrow morning, my pet, we'll have a little honeymoon," Henderson said. "Just a few weeks on the Riviera. You'll be outstanding there, my pet; I'll be so proud of you."

Rosa leaned forward and pressed his knee.

"And you will really be able to forget all the unpleasant things that have happened to you, my dear." Henderson put down his cup and saucer, stood up, went across to her, and kissed her lightly on the forehead. "Now I must go upstairs for a little while—clearing up, you know, clearing up. Mustn't neglect business, I've another mouth to feed now!"

He patted her cheek, and went out of the room, leaving Rosa looking as if she were satiated with joy.

He went upstairs to the study. The black-clad manservant was waiting there for him. He closed the door before speaking.

"Well?"

"Not a squeak," said the manservant. "I can almost believe he doesn't know where the plates are."

"If he doesn't, his brother does."

"We'll soon see, Boss."

"Yes." Henderson walked across to the wall, where a bookcase stood as high as the top of the oak panelling. "I'll have a word with the young fool myself."

He stretched up and pressed a button in one of the shelves, and the bookcase moved away from the wall on an automatic swivel. A dark space showed up inside—a little cubby hole, no more than six feet square.

As the light from the study shone in, Richard's face appeared; and then Kathleen's. They were standing in opposite corners, a few feet away from each other. They were tied by the wrists to hooks in the wall, and couldn't move close enough to touch each other.

RICHARD raised his head as the light fell on his face. His chin was thrust out, and he looked defiant, almost aggressive—but he also shot an anxious glance at the girl. She was sagging from the hook, and her eyes were filled with dread—dread of what had happened and of what might come. She wore the clothes she had on on the morning of her disappearance, rumpled and dusty. Her hair was dishevelled. In spite of that, the beauty showed through; and courage.

Richard, unshaven, pale from the pain in his leg, looked calmly back at Henderson.

"Having a nice time?" Henderson asked sneeringly. "So near and yet so far—wouldn't you have enjoyed yourself if I'd given you a few more inches of rope, Fane?"

Richard didn't answer.

"Lost your tongue?" Henderson raised his fist and snapped his fingers under Richard's nose. "You'd better find it. Where are the plates?"

"I've told you that I don't know."

"I've told you I don't believe you."

Richard said, "I can't hammer it into your thick head."

"Richard——" began Kathleen.

Henderson went across to her, ran his hand caressingly over her face, over her shoulders. Then he bent forward and kissed her—she couldn't move to avoid his lips. Richard watched, and his pallor faded into a dusky red; there was murder in his eyes.

Henderson stood back—and slapped Kathleen's face.

"You swine——" Richard choked.

" Don't you like having lessons? " asked Henderson softly. " You'll have to put up with a lot more, if you don't tell me where the plates are, Fane. You've got yourself a nice little filly, but you're not the only one who thinks she's nice. Don't forget it, you fool. Where are they? "

" *I don't know !* "

Henderson said, " If you don't, your brother does. And if he doesn't see sense I'll bring him here. You wouldn't like that, would you? Two's company, three's a crowd."

He stretched out his hand, pulled Kathleen's hair sharply, then deliberately raised his foot and kicked Richard in the pit of the stomach. Richard gasped and tried involuntarily to double up; but couldn't.

Henderson laughed.

" You'll find out what it's like to be hurt if I don't get the plates to-night."

He went out, and the manservant, who had watched impassively from the opening, pushed the bookcase back into position, shutting the prisoners up in darkness. Henderson lit a cigarette and sat down at his desk. He was scowling.

" I see what you mean. He wouldn't stand that if he knew. Or would he? "

" I don't think he knows." The manservant stood at ease, in front of the desk. " Boss, I'm wondering if you could have made a mistake."

Henderson didn't speak, but the silence invited the other to go on.

" I'm wondering if Hicky got hold of them."

" What makes you think he might have? "

" If Fane doesn't know where the plates are, he didn't take them. You always thought he did. When he started calling at Number Six you began to get worried. The plates were taken out of the flat at Number Five when he was across the way. You know that, that's what first started you thinking about him. Rosa told you he was often there, didn't she? She used to go out for the evening and let the love-birds have the flat. Remember?"

"Don't talk to me like a parrot. Of course I remember."

"Okay, then." The manservant wasn't perturbed by that rebuke. "Supposing it was Hicky. He tried to double-cross over the slush in Number Five, didn't he? Thanks to him we lost the lot. And he knew you were going to double-cross him—Ben and I heard him tell Fane that before I shot him. Why couldn't he have taken the plates before, and salted them away?"

Henderson shook his head.

"It wasn't Hicky," he said emphatically. "He didn't try any double-cross until after he was nearly caught with the ashes. He thought we'd framed him for that, and that's what made him turn and try to get the slush from the other flat for himself. As it happened his time was up by then. But I'm sure the Fanes have got the plates."

"Okay, so they've got them." The manservant shrugged. "We'll soon know, Ben ought to ring up by five-fifteen, didn't he? But supposing he *hasn't* got them? Supposing we've been wrong about the Fanes? Supposing Richard's right when he says he doesn't know where the stuff is? What will that add up to, Boss?" When Henderson didn't answer, the man leaned forward and said softly, "That Hicky had it and salted it away somewhere."

Henderson said, "You're all wrong. The Fanes are in it. They'll hand over the plates because they think it will save Richard's life. What a hope!"

He looked at his watch; it was five minutes past five.

The manservant said, "Better be careful where you rub them out, Boss. We don't want trouble here. I agree they've got to go because they know all about you now, but we'd better get them a long way from here."

"We'll fix it safely," said Henderson.

He lit another cigarette, stood up, and began to pace

204

the room. The manservant still stood by impassively. There was no sound in the study—nothing to suggest that Richard and Kathleen were behind the bookcase and could hear every word. A car passed along the road, but there was nothing else except the faint ticking of a clock.

" Take it easy," the manservant said. " We'll get through, Boss. Even if we don't get the plates we can clear with what we have got. We won't do so badly. Just take it easy."

Henderson glared at him, and began to pace to and fro again—and the telephone bell rang.

Henderson's hand moved towards it and then hovered above it. The manservant licked his lips. Henderson plucked the instrument from the cradle.

" *Hallo ?* "

The manservant saw his tension, the knuckles white as he gripped the receiver, and his face set; then relaxation set in, he moved round slowly, sat in his chair, and the receiver almost slipped from his grasp.

After a pause he said, " Fine, fine! Don't bring them here, make sure you're not followed, and then call me again."

He replaced the receiver, wiped his forehead, and then grinned at the manservant; it was meant to be sarcastic, but his relief was too great for that, it simply showed his delight.

" He's got them," he breathed. " Old Man Fane turned up. Says Martin's hurt his foot. I don't care what Martin's hurt, he hasn't hurt us! "

" That's fine, Boss."

" And was I right? " asked Henderson. He gave a little cackle of a laugh. " Now we can get moving. As soon as we're sure that Ben wasn't followed, we'll collect the plates. The aeroplane's ready, and we'll get out of the country, I've got all the necessary papers. If everything blows over, fine, I can come back here. If it doesn't——"

" It'll be okay," said the manservant. " I'm glad you were right, Boss."

"I'm *always* right," said Henderson. He stood up, wiped his forehead again, and then turned towards the bookcase. "Now we can deal with that pair."

It was twenty-five minutes past five.

.　　　.　　　.　　　.　　　.

Martin had not been followed.

He made sure of that, in the early afternoon, while walking about the West End. Neither the police nor the crooks showed any interest in him. He'd heard nothing more from Kelby; the plans made with his father were to be put into operation. At four o'clock he went on to a garage where he was known, and hired an old but fast Riley. He was on the outskirts of Wimbledon by twenty to five. He parked the car in a wide street, half a mile from Common Rise, and walked up and down, smoking two cigarettes in quick succession. His nerves were almost shrieking.

At five o'clock he went back to the car and drove to the Corner of Common Rise. He left the car round the corner. In the wide street there were a few lamps, but none of them shone brightly, and none was near The Beams. He didn't let himself think too much of what had brought him here; now and again he smiled, always at the thought of Rennie. The smile soon vanished, in acute anxiety for Richard and Kathleen.

He reached the gateway of The Beams and walked past. A light burned in the porch; that was a pity. He studied the house while standing to one side, at the gates; that showed him that the right-hand side was darkness—the front door wasn't in the middle, but towards the left. There was a ground-floor room with light streaming out on the right. He slipped into the garden and walked round towards the left side of the house. But for the light at the porch it would have been pitch dark; and it was cold. He walked on grass most of the time, but now and again had to step across a gravel path; the noise he made seemed loud.

206

Soon he was at the side of the house, looking at the windows. There was no sound anywhere, except a faint rustle of the leaves in the bushes. He examined the nearest window; it was shut tightly, and when he shone his torch, he saw that it was latched.

He moved to the next.

He couldn't even be sure that Richard was here. For the first time since he had left London the possibility that Rennie was playing some deep, double game flashed into his mind; once in, it wouldn't go out.

The second window was open an inch at the top.

He couldn't reach the top, even when standing at his full height, so he moved away, looking round the shrubbery and at a small shed; he found nothing to stand on here. He tried the door of the shed; it wasn't locked. A garden-seat stood just inside, light enough for him to carry. He took it to the window, and when standing on it he could get at the window without difficulty. He pushed it down; it made a little squeaking noise, that was all. He examined it closely, and found that the lower pane was fastened by a special catch; he would have to climb through the top, and that wouldn't be easy.

He shone his torch into the room; it was small, looked like a morning-room. There were easy-chairs and oddments of furniture, and a small table beneath the window, with a vase of flowers on it. He stood on the back of the garden-seat, and put his leg through the gap. It seemed an age before he was able to touch the table, and when he did he kicked the vase. It rocked—and fell. It didn't make much noise on the carpet, but much more than he liked. He drew his other leg in, and climbed down from the table. Triumph at forcing entry was lost in anxiety.

He went towards the door, and as he reached it he heard footsteps. He flattened himself against the wall. The door opened, light streamed in, and Rosa came into the room.

Rosa didn't see him.

She switched on the light and stared towards the flower-vase, lying in a pool of water, with the flowers strewn about, and then glanced at the window. She must have realized in a moment what it meant. She stood with her hands raised, her mouth open—and might let out the single scream which would bring others running. Martin went forward, hands outstretched. She heard something, turned, a scream started from her lips—and then his fingers closed round her throat.

She made a gurgling sound, and kicked at him; she caught him painfully on the shin, but he didn't let go. Her arms whirled round like flails, but he held her at arm's length and she couldn't touch him. He saw her eyes, rounded, staring, and her lips wide open as she struggled for breath. Her body heaved and writhed. She was losing consciousness and fighting against it, but she wouldn't be able to fight for long.

Her body began to sag.

He didn't want to kill her, was already afraid that he had held her for too long. He released his pressure, and she fell slowly to the floor. He broke her fall, laid her out straight, and then felt her pulse; she was breathing. Time was precious, but he didn't dare leave her yet, she might die on his hands.

He waited for two minutes. Then he could see her breast moving, as she breathed. He stuffed a handkerchief into her mouth, and looked round for something with which to tie her hands and feet; nothing was handy. He took off his tie and fastened her hands behind her back, and told himself he hadn't served any of the real apprenticeship yet; every time he did something he realized how much he lacked.

He stood back, then lifted her bodily and put her behind a large easy-chair behind the door. No one who happened to pass would see her. He hesitated, then righted the vase and picked up the flowers; every second was vital, but he wanted to make sure he didn't betray his presence too easily. He put the flowers back without trying to arrange them, and then pushed up the window.

He went into the passage and closed the door.

It was very quiet.

The passage led to the hall and the staircase. He walked along softly; the carpet muffled every sound of his approach. He paused at the foot of the stairs. A door stood open, and a bright light shone through. He peered into the drawing-room, and found that it was empty.

He went upstairs, knowing exactly where he would find the study.

The door was closed.

He didn't know why he looked at his watch; partly, perhaps, because he had timed this by guesswork and his guessing might be all wrong.

It was half-past five.

Barbara would be telephoning Scotland Yard now, and giving them this address. If they contacted the local police, some would be here in ten minutes; possibly in less. He might not have sufficient time. There was a light beneath the study door.

He stepped towards it cautiously, and took out the gun—the dead man's gun. He kept it in his right hand, and turned the handle of the door slowly and silently.

He heard a voice; Henderson's.

" Still having a nice time, Fane? "

.   .   .   .   .

Martin drew back, gritting his teeth. It was absurd, and afterwards he knew that it had lost vital seconds, but the effect was like a punch to the jaw; a kind of shocked relief. He now knew for certain that this was the end of the hunt. He found his forehead and his neck clammy cold. He wiped his forehead with the back of his left hand as Henderson spoke again.

"Hear our little conversation, did you? You know what's going to happen, then. We've got the plates, your brother had them after all. And you said you didn't know."

Martin pushed the door an inch.

Richard said in a voice which hardly carried, "You ruddy fool, Clarke. Martin hasn't got them, and doesn't know where they are, any more than I do."

.   .   .   .   .

Martin heard a sound that might have been a hissing intake of breath. He didn't move, couldn't yet see into the room. The silence seemed electric.

Henderson was Clarke.

No, that was nonsense; Richard didn't know that Clarke's body was in the garage at Nairn Lodge.

Henderson said thinly, "That's a lie, Fane. We've collected the plates, we've just had a message."

"Then Scoop fooled you," Richard said. He actually laughed, and spoke as if he were talking to himself. "Scoop or the Maestro, I wouldn't like to guess which. You're just a fool, Henderson."

Henderson said, "If you think you can save yourself that way——"

A girl screamed.

Martin pushed open the door.

Henderson and the manservant stood with their backs to him, facing what looked like a hole in the wall. He couldn't see Richard. He could see that the bookcase was out of its position; it was like a book-lined door.

"Take it easy, Kath," Richard said. "We'll get through."

There was a knife in Clarke's hand. Martin saw it glint, as he moved forward, and realized what Henderson

—Henderson?—had planned. Neither of the men knew he was behind them. He still couldn't see Richard, although he thought he could make out the pale blur of a face in the darkness beyond the hole in the wall.

Henderson said, " Okay." He moved forward. " I'll stick this knife into the girl. Where it will hurt. And I'll keep doing it, unless you tell me where to get those plates. Understand? " He was outlined against the darkness of the little cubby hole now, and the knife was out of sight. " Don't get it wrong, Fane. You've both had it. You know too much to live, but I'll make it a quick death if you come across. Where are the plates? "

" Clarke——" There was a desperate note in Richard's voice. " Don't kill Kath. She——"

" I'll hurt her all right."

Clarke moved a step forward.

" Hallo," said Martin mildly.

Clarke and the manservant swung round. Clarke raised the knife, as if to throw. Martin shot him in the shoulder. The manservant leapt at him; Martin shot him in the chest. Clarke reeled back against the wall, the other man fell to the floor. The knife lay on the carpet, glistening. Martin stepped forward, and Richard cried out in an unbelieving voice:

" Scoop! "

" I won't be long, old chap," said Martin. He went to Henderson-Clarke, who was unconscious, and felt in his pocket and beneath his coat; he wasn't carrying a gun; nor was the manservant. Martin picked Clarke up and dumped him in a chair, then went into the cubby-hole. There was a light switch; he pressed it down, saw the hooks and the cords. He went back for the knife, and began to release them, starting with the girl.

.   .   .   .   .

When they were free he carried the two prisoners into another room; each was hurt enough to be disabled. He locked the door on them and went back to the others.

.   .   .   .   .

Kathleen sat back in the desk chair, her eyes closed. Martin gave her a little brandy, from a bottle and glass in a cupboard, and Richard watched intently as she swallowed. She hadn't spoken since she had been released. Richard, looking pale and sick with pain, forced a smile and held out his hand for the glass. When he took it he dropped it, and brandy spilled over his legs.

" Shocking waste," he muttered. " Feed me. Sorry."

Martin picked up the glass, refilled it and put it to his lips; Richard took a little, and licked his lips slowly. His eyes were clouded as if with pain.

" Where's the main trouble, Skip? " Martin asked.

" Leg. It'll be all right. Been standing on it since they brought me here. You alone? "

" The police will be here soon."

" Kelby, I hope." Richard grinned faintly. " It ought to give him a shock. Had you—twigged it? "

" What? "

" Henderson being Clarke."

" I thought that Clarke——"

" Was the chap in the garage," said Richard. " Not on your life! " His voice was husky with fatigue, but he was anxious to talk. " We could hear everything in our little dungeon. They employed a man who looked like Clarke—employed him because he was rather the same build, face, and figure. Killed him and dumped him in the garage, because they thought that would make us cough up. Henderson is Clarke. Double-life chap. As Clarke, married to his Emma, leaving her alone most of the time. As Clarke, working in his paper business. He was smart—used rubber cheek pads, made himself look plumper than he was, dressed differently. The real man is in the other room. He had always planned to make Clarke disappear, and to bob up as the reputable Mr. Henderson, who made money out of films. I——"

" Leave this, until you've had some rest," Martin advised.

" Not yet. I want to tell you, and then sleep. How

I want to sleep!" Richard was making a tremendous effort to keep his voice steady. "As Clarke he ran the forgery gang. His wife discovered what he was up to—and she threatened to tell the police. So—he killed her. He tried to burn the corpse, but found it wasn't so easy as he had thought. Then he had a brain-wave. If he let the body be identifiable, then killed the man who resembled him, it would look like murder followed by suicide. So he dumped his wife's body in the river, making sure the sack was rotten and the face and body looked as if someone had tried to prevent identification."

"And left the bracelet with the name on—that was always too easy, if we'd only had the sense to see it," said Martin.

"Of course. After this he went back to Buckley Street, and the idea was that Hicky would get the man who looked like Clarke to go along there and be killed and faked up as a suicide. But it didn't work out, because when Henderson-Clarke started packing up he found that the plates were missing from their hiding-place in the flat. Playing for time, he called off the suicide stunt and told Hicky to collect the ashes that night. He didn't want the police in Buckley Street until he'd found the plates. But, of course, the police were already on his track. They nearly caught Hicky, but Henderson had him killed the next day. The men were down at Wapping before I got there. They didn't try to kill me, by the way—that shot was to show me they meant business.

"Meanwhile Hicky thought they had double-crossed him by tipping off the police when he went to get the ashes, so he tried to snatch the slush from Number Six the next day. If it hadn't been for you he'd have got away with it—though it wouldn't have done him any good. Henderson had planned the same thing, and got the two girls out of the flat—and then Hicky's men walked in.

"Henderson had put the stuff under the floorboards in Number Six a long time before. He knew there was always the danger of the police getting on to him as Clarke and making a raid."

" Did Rosa——"

" Rosa knew nothing. He was careful that she should never see him as Clarke—and at the same time he cultivated her through the Licker Club. It was clever. He got her to talk about her life at the flat, and knew when Kath would be out. He would take Rosa out at the same time—and the slush went under the floorboards. It was easy for him to get a wax impression of Rosa's key. Rosa still doesn't know—doesn't even know that Kath and I are in this house. Of course he cooked his own goose there in the end—fell for her lush figure, and finally married her. Perhaps he fancied that this way she would keep quiet if she did suspect anything—and anyhow, a wife can't be called to give evidence against her husband. But she never knew he was Clarke. I'm almost sorry for poor Rosa."

" The Peke——"

" Ching was really Henderson's undoing, I suppose. It was in the flat when he killed Mrs. Clarke—he didn't know that until too late. Ching started yapping, and he chased it round the room. Can't you imagine how mad he was? But it kept dodging, and when he opened the front door it didn't stop running till it lost itself in the Strand. Then it was picked up and taken to the pet shop. He was so mad that he went off the handle when Kath asked him about Ching the next day. Kath was kidnapped, of course, because she knew too much—though she didn't know it! She had seen him as Clarke, could recognize him—the only person who could. He phoned her up as Henderson, told her he had a big film part in mind for her, and—well, the rest was easy."

" And the body in the garage at Nairn Lodge? " asked Martin. " That was Clarke's double, you say? "

" Yes, when the suicide plan didn't work out he decided to make it look as if we'd killed Clarke—that was all part of his plan to get the plates."

" Richard, do you know where these plates are? "

" I haven't a clue." Richard forced a laugh. " He suspected me because I was sometimes alone with Kath in the flat opposite, and he couldn't think of anyone else. I suppose it must have been Hicky. Perhaps one day the police——"

He paused.

There was a thunderous knocking at a door downstairs.

J ONATHAN F ANE sat at Martin's desk at the office.   Evelyn
was in the client's chair; Barbara had brought in a chair
from the other small office.   The Yard had been told
everything; no news had come through, and it was after
six o'clock.   Evelyn sat like a statue, her face pale and her
eyes very bright.   Fane smoked cigarette after cigarette.

The telephone bell rang.

Barbara, farther away, reached the instrument first, and
Fane's hand closed over hers, but he took it away and
she picked up the receiver.   Evelyn turned her head
towards the telephone and held her breath.

" Hal—hallo," Barbara gasped.

" Scoop! " she cried.

" *Are they all right?* " breathed Evelyn.

Fane closed his eyes and pressed his hand against his
forehead.   Evelyn went to Barbara's side, and looked as
if she would tear the receiver out of her grasp.

Barbara listened, and kept saying in asides:

" *Richard's safe. . . . So is Kath . . . No one's hurt . . .
Henderson was Clarke. . . .*"

She spoke more quietly into the telephone:

" Yes, darling, we'll go to your flat.   Come as soon as
you can."

She rang off.

" Thank God for that," breathed Evelyn.   " Thank
God for that."

She went across to Fane, her hand held out.   He put a
handkerchief into it, and she dabbed at her eyes and nose ;
Barbara was also sniffing.   Fane's eyes looked suspiciously
moist, and he cleared his throat noisily before he
spoke.

" Better get to the flat. They'll be hungry. I'll go
down and get a taxi."

" We—we don't want a taxi," snuffled Evelyn. " We
can walk. All you can think about is—is—taxis!"
She caught her breath and then began to cry.

Fane went downstairs and called a taxi.

.   .   .   .   .

The Fane family were at the Leyden Lane flat, a little
over two hours later. Richard sat in a chair with his
leg on the pouf—every available chair had been pressed
into service. Barbara's delicatessen friend had come up
to scratch again. Martin had done most of the talking;
Richard had added a word here and there. The only
one of the party of six who didn't speak, after a first
greeting, was Kathleen Wilder.

Evelyn kept glancing at her. Kathleen hadn't changed
her clothes, but she looked much more herself, had done
her hair and made up.

Her eyes were heavy with fatigue as she listened to
Martin.

" After Richard told me the story, the police arrived,"
Martin ended. " Kelby was there half an hour after
the local people. Quite civil, too, even after I'd made a
full confession about finding that body in the garage."
Martin smiled reflectively. " I don't think he's a bad
chap, when you get to know him! The police had
followed Henderson-Clarke's other man, who'd taken the
stuff from you, Dad, and picked him up. Kelby admitted
that if we hadn't taken our line Richard and Kathleen
might have been killed.

" He knew about Clarke's double identity, by the way—
at least, suspected Clarke had another identity, and was
expecting a body to turn up. The only delicate ground
will be explaining away our lie about why I went to the
Lodge, but——" He shrugged. " I don't think Kelby
will make much of a point of that."

" He'd better not," said Evelyn.

217

Richard yawned.

"And believe it or not, he's got the missing plates. Mrs. Clarke had found them and sent them to her parents. She'd told them to hold them in an unopened parcel. When they'd recovered from the shock of knowing she had been murdered, they thought of the parcel and gave it to the police."

"Well, well!" Richard yawned again.

"It's absurd to sit up any longer," Evelyn said. "You *must* get to bed, Skip. And Kathleen—Kathleen, I'm so sorry about all you've been through, my dear. I'm looking forward to getting to know you. I wonder if you'd like to have Richard's room at the Lasil Street Hotel? Or——"

"Kathleen's coming home with me," insisted Barbara. "I must go and send Jessica home soon, too, or Rennie will think we've kidnapped her. Nothing will be too good for Rennie," she added thoughtfully. "I suppose we can decide what to do about him in the morning."

Martin laughed; and it was good to hear.

"We've decided! He's coming on the staff—Prince would approve, I think, Dad. He'll be an invaluable contact man. It will probably upset Kelby, but——"

"Who cares?" asked Richard, and yawned again.

"I'll drive you round to your flat, then," Martin said to Barbara. "I can take Jessica home, too. If you'll stay here until we get back," he added to his parents, "I'll run you to Lasil Street. We could all do with an early night."

"Very well," said Evelyn. "But one thing's certain, and I won't hear a word against it. To-morrow we're *all* going to Dorset. We can have a few days' rest. If the police want us——"

"Better make it next week-end," advised Fane. "Richard ought to have a few days in bed before he travels. Everyone will enjoy it more then, too."

Evelyn glared at him. He went across to her, took her in his arms and, lipstick notwithstanding, kissed her full on the lips.

"Oh, you fool!" she said.
"Let that be a lesson to us, Scoop," said Richard.
"Kath—come here!"

. . . . .

Martin and Barbara sat alone in the office in the Strand on the following Wednesday morning. The sensation had died down, but on the clients' list at Prince there were already a hundred names. It was nearly lunch-time, and there was a lull in the numbers of callers.

Jessica was out at lunch. She had proved surprisingly capable at handling callers, had a business-like but helpful manner which pleased most of them. Rennie was already out on one or two inquiries, including the quest of a certain gold watch. Kelby had been told what was to happen and had made no comments. All of them had made statements to the police; all had been warned that they would be wanted at the trial as witnesses. Henderson and Ben, who had been picked up after taking the parcel from Fane at Piccadilly, had each been before the magistrate and remanded for eight days in custody. The manservant was in hospital and would be charged later.

"As soon as Jessica's back we'll go and get some lunch," Martin said. "I get hungrier every day."

"I'm hungry." Barbara pushed a few strands of hair from her forehead. "Darling, what a crazy business it all was! There's one good thing, I got to know your mother and father as I probably wouldn't know them in years. I honestly don't know which one I like best."

Martin chuckled.

"I rate them evens, too."

The telephone rang as he finished. He lifted it, and said:

"Prince speaking."

Suddenly he grinned; then he chuckled, and said:

"Wonderful! Bring it round this afternoon." He rang off, and his eyes were shining. "Rennie's got that gold watch. It fell out of the man's pocket, and the bus conductor was tempted. He fell. Rennie persuaded him to hand it over."

Barbara said, " Our first success! "

" First! "

They laughed gaily—and the buzzer buzzed loudly. Martin went to see who it was. He saw a man's back, and realized that two men were carrying something into the office. As they drew nearer he saw that it was a folded carpet.

" Bar! " he cried.

Barbara came hurrying, and stopped abruptly.

" Good gracious! *Carpet*. Did you——"

" Lady ordered it yesterday, said it must be in to-day," said one of the men, gruffly. " One for each room, this is for the big one. Drop your end, Mick. Have to move the desks, guv'nor."

Martin didn't anwer; he was too surprised.

" Of—of course," said Barbara, and took Martin's hand. " Scoop, we'll send her a telegram, with luck it'll arrive before they get home. How shall we word it? "

Martin was beaming.

" Eh? Oh—I don't know. Dad would know. What about this? ' Carpets, carpets everywhere and not a board to trip.' "

" Wonderful! And we'll add just a word or two, and——"

" *Do* you mind if we move the desks? " demanded the carpet man impatiently.

· · · · ·

Just after lunch on the following Saturday the Buick turned into the drive at Nairn Lodge. Martin was driving, Barbara sat next to him. Richard and Kathleen were at the back, and Kathleen looked as fresh and lovely as the warm spring day. The daffodils had come out under the warming influence of two days' sun, the lawns were perfect, the square Georgian simplicity of the house had a charm of its own. Sampson was standing near the porch, Evelyn Fane was coming out of the front door.

" Here we are," said Richard. " Don't worry, sweet, it won't be an ordeal."

Barbara and Martin were already out of the car, and Evelyn was hurrying forward. Richard, limping slightly, helped Kathleen out. There was a moment of silence—not awkward, but noticeable; and in it there came the sound of tapping.

Kathleen's eyes widened, and she glanced up at an open window.

" Your father's secretary *can* type," she said.

Richard grinned, Martin winked, Barbara chuckled, and Evelyn shot a long-suffering glance towards the window, and said :

" Darling! Stop that typing and come down, they're here. Kathleen already thinks you're your own secretary, she can't believe you'd work all the hours there are."

A deep voice called, " Two minutes, darling! "

" Two minutes—it's always two minutes," said Evelyn. " Bless him! Kathleen, I'm really glad you're here."

The brothers Fane exchanged glances; contented glances.